THE GENTLEMAN OF D-BLOCK 3

Rabbit Season

SA'ID SALAAM

Urban Aesop Publicatons

All praise is to Allah. Peace be upon His final prophet and all those who follow the guidance. I dedicate this one to myself for staying true to myself and my Lord.

Synopsis

The explosive finale of The Gentlemen of D-Block is here.

It ain't no fun when the rabbit has the gun and Rabbit is clearly winning in D-Block. Old beefs create new dangers for Rabbit and company not to mention internal strife amongst his team threatens his reign. Next a dangerous new inmate arrives and sets his sights on Rabbit, as well.

Heavy is the head that wears the crown and the pressure is starting to wear Trouble down. Between balancing his operations, gang and family life he's pulled in different directions. No man has two hearts so he'll have to chose

Rollo and his Rollers are gaining in numbers and threaten to become the dominant gang in the facility. Malaysia made her choice but can she handle the repercussions of it. Will Trouble respect it of will there be trouble.

One eyed Dino is still plotting on avenging the eye he lost twenty years earlier. Once a new source comes along he no longer needs Rabbit. The failed hit means he has to do it himself. The Gentlemen of D-Block 3, Rabbit Season.

Chapter One

"*A*we man..." Pablo groaned when he awoke to find his wet dream was no dream at all. If it wasn't a dream then he really did fuck his partner's girl, well.

"Mmhm!" Malaysia laughed at his predicament. "Yeah you did. We did. A 'coupla times!"

"At least," he said seeing the empty three pack condom box on the night stand. He had fucked his partner's girl three times.

'He said look out for her, you looked out for her by making her cum' the devil suggested like the devil suggest *'May as well fuck her again'*

"Mm-mm," Pablo declined, shaking his head.

"Let me find out you crazy! Talking to yourself," she laughed and pulled him back into the present. That led them to the awkward moment as they contemplated whether or not they should fuck again. They could blame the weed and alcohol for last night but both were dead sober at the moment.

"Man..." He sighed again and rolled towards her. She rolled and met him halfway so their tongues could meet once again. He let out a guttural moan when she gripped his throbbing dick. "Ion got no more rubbers!"

"Don't, come, in me, then," she advised as she rolled him onto his back. Any protest he may have had dropped dead when she mounted him then reached down and rubbed his swollen dick against her slippery box. It was so slippery it slipped inside. She sank slowly down the shaft, gripping the dick with her tight walls.

Pablo leaned up and took a nipple in his mouth as Malaysia searched for a stroke. She found one and slowly rocked on the dick while he gripped her round ass. He changed nipples every few seconds while she rocked. Rocked and hissed, rocked and moaned.

"Get up!" He urged when the rocking, hissing and moaning got the better of him.

"Huh?" She asked in between a rock and a hiss and he exploded inside of her. "Oh."

Malaysia giggled as he squirmed beneath her. She felt a sense of power when he reacted each time she contracted her muscles and squeezed the dick. Luckily for both she had continued taking her birth control pills even after Trouble went to jail.

"Glad, you think, it's, funny," he remarked and wiggled under her. "Get up so we can get something to eat."

"I cain't. I gotta make a trip," she whined but did ease off the dick just as she had eased on it. She would have loved to stay right there, with him deep up inside of her, but had a previous engagement.

"Where you going so early?" He asked as if he had a right to. Her face gave part of the answer before her mouth opened and gave the rest.

"To see Trouble," she admitted and pulled her panties on. Malaysia would have loved a shower and fresh underwear but that meant going home, which meant being late. She only got to see Trouble two days a week and he liked to spend every minute of visitation hours with her.

Pablo walked Malaysia out to her car and slobbed her down before she got in. He wanted to tell her to stay but didn't. She would have, had he, but he didn't. They had business to handle for now so she pulled out of the driveway and pulled away.

Malaysia didn't even turn the radio on during the long

ride. She enjoyed the gentle throb of her sore vagina and how it got like that. What goes up, does come down including come and she squirmed in her seat. After fussing Jaquita out it was her who leaked on the leather seats.

"Dang!" Malaysia fussed at the passersby who passed by her changing in the prison parking lot. She could have changed at Pablo's house but felt some kind of way at being Pablo's house. It wasn't exactly guilt since she planned to spend many more nights at Pablo's house.

She had learned to keep prison appropriate clothing in the trunk to cut down of trips to the dollar store. It wasn't the few bucks she spent but the frumpy selection that got her. Last night was a night of firsts, but today brought on a new first as well. A deep sigh escaped when she joined the line near the end. She usually arrived earlier enough to be up front but for the first time she didn't want to be here.

"Hey there," the regular officer greeted as he checked her in. He recognized the look in her eyes even if she didn't recognize it in her heart yet.

"Hey," Malaysia moaned like she didn't want to be here. The drive was extra long today. Her vagina was still tingling from the good loving she got as a good morning. That made the ride even longer and caused her to fight not to turn around every other exit.

Malaysia cleared the metal detectors and made her way over to the visitation room. Her head shook at the half empty machines so early as she got what she could. Trouble was seated at the table by the time she returned to the table with some hot food and cold drinks.

"Sup shawty," he said stoically and stood.

"Oh hey," Malaysia greeted with the tone of bumping into an acquaintance in the Piggly Wiggly, instead of driving two hours. She turned her cheek when he leaned in for a hug and kiss. It seemed like a slight but it was actually respectful since she had the next man in her mouth a few hours ago. It was indeed a night of first and her first sixty nine had her eager for a second.

"OK then," he said just to acknowledge the curb. The hot

double burger prevented any further talk on the matter. He was in the middle of the sandwich when he mumbled, "You gave it to Pablo?"

"Who!" She reeled defensively. She didn't want to lie to him but wasn't ready for the truth either. She was taken by Pablo but didn't know if he felt the same.

"You, the money. You got that to him?" He explained just short of her confession. He hadn't called either this morning since the recent murders had the prison on edge.

"Oh yeah! The money!" She practically cheered. "Mmhm, he got it."

Trouble nodded as he polished off the burger and unwrapped his chicken sandwich. Malaysia got a kick out of his scarfing his food down and cracked a smile. Trouble was smiling as well since he had a play in motion that would make them rich. Not to mention another round inside the round Miss Jessie. He always heard big girls got thee best pussy and now he knew it for a fact.

"What?" Malaysia questioned his smirk. Despite wearing one of her own thinking about the night she spent with Pablo. He was so pretty to her she had turned her head and watched while he delivered solid back shots. She even cheered him on withe chants of 'get that pussy'.

"Thinking about this lil move! The whole damn camp on the cream!" He exclaimed. It was an exaggeration but not too far from the truth.

Methamphetamine had certainly become the drug of choice among the prisoners. They may have separated and divided themselves by race, language and gang, but meth was the common denominator. The Rollers were already raising havoc but being both addicted and broke fueled their Viking like raids throughout the prison.

Meth has long been dubbed the gay man's drug so it was no surprise that most of the Bandos were users. The Mexicans, the White Boys, civilians and some Riders as well. Trouble spoke down on the drug but couldn't ban it because that's how some people chose to do their time. The judges gave the time but its up to each individual to figure out how to do it.

Some dudes do their time watching sports or arguing about sports. Others played sports and or worked out. Some slept with men until they could get home to their wives or girlfriends. Some of them brought a deadly virus home to those same wives or girlfriends.

Some pretended to be Muslim or Christians to do their time. Some of them dibbled and dabbled in drugs or even homosexuality since they weren't sincere. Some were sincere and still had those issues.

Sa'id usually had a zero tolerance stance on drugs but for once he wasn't in charge. The religion teaches that whoever sees an evil must change it with their hand, or speech or at the very least hate it in their heart. The latter was the least but that's all he had left at the moment.

Jahil was knee deep in the prison drug trade as well as other things. What's done in the dark usually comes to the light and exposes the secrets. He used Friday prayers, as well as members of the community to do his distribution.

"That's nice," she replied and pulled him from his thoughts. They had been so close for so long she wanted to share her good news. But since that entailed sharing her good pussy with his friend she kept it to herself.

"So, what y'all seen?" He asked since they were supposed to hit a movie.

"The Dark Prince, but I fell asleep a few minutes after it started," she recalled. It was a good answer since he watched it on his phone and she wouldn't have been able to recall a single scene. A movie about a vampire who is a rapper is not something easily forgotten.

"Missed a good one," he sighed. Something had changed but he couldn't put a finger on it. The visit passed with small talk and current events from the hood.

"I'll have to, Mmhm, yeah," she rambled with her mind elsewhere while she scanned the large room. They both settled on a man with his family nearby.

"Bruh right there be here err weekend with his wife and

kids, but be messing with boys in the dorm," Trouble said shaking his head. He knew the man from the dorm and knew he kept a pet fuck boy. His wife had no idea he was using her money to support his 'shim'.

"Just nasty," Malaysia moaned. Nothing like the way she moaned last night while doing the nasty with Pablo. Her vagina throbbed again at the thought of him inside of her. Trouble's lips were moving but she didn't hear the words. "Mmhm, oh Ok. Mmhm."

Malaysia had drank enough soda to wash the dick traces from her mouth so he was able to get a proper kiss by the time it was time to go. Even though they haven't made enough soda to wash all the dick out since it's the thought that counts. Essence of the dick still remains and that's too much. It was a good kiss too and he would have won her back if he could have left with her. He couldn't though for at least a few more years and the young girl didn't have them in her.

"Brang my son next time you come," he insisted as they broke off their embrace.

"Who! No I didn't!" She said defensively since all she heard was the word come. Her mind had slipped off to last night when she came on the tip of Pablo's tongue.

"Trevor? Our son?" He reminded since he couldn't read minds. He could read body language and knew something had changed.

"Oh, Ok. Yeah," she agreed with a sigh of relief. Malaysia hadn't needed to be deceptive much in her young life and wasn't very good at it. Young girls like her fall in and out of love like an Alicia Keys song so her heart had moved on already.

"Yeah, Ok, um yeah, bye," he said awkwardly, then watched her round ass shift away. He stood on line to be stripped searched as all prisoners are when returning from visit.

Some officers had no desire to look under nut sacks or up anuses and just gave a quick pat down. Some officers did like to look under nut sacks and up anuses, so they did. Common sense dictates that if a man, put anything up his ass, he must really want it. The warden insisted all inmates be thoroughly searched to ensure her drugs were the only drugs coming into the prison.

"Sup Clayton," the officer assigned to check under nut sacks and up anuses greeted when Trouble reached his station.

"Same shit, different day," he said as he was patted down while still fully dressed. The officer was on the warden's payroll so knew he wouldn't be smuggling anything in this way. He rushed back to the dorm to check on his new way in.

Chapter Two

"**S**hit," Pablo said when he saw the name on his screen. This was a conversation he wasn't particularly looking forward to but business was business, so he took the call. "Ride or die shit!"

"Facts!" Trouble cheered like he believed it. The gang could ride or die all they liked. His agenda was to keep stacking his bread and bounce. "You took care of that?"

"I'm just getting down here now. 'Spouse to meet yo peeps in five," he said as the GPS directed him to a trailer park.

"Cool. I'll hang out with you then," Trouble said and stayed on the line. "Y'all checked a movie last night?"

"I did. Yo girl was slobbering in her popcorn!" Pablo said, as rehearsed. He had even checked out the movie that morning in preparation for a pop quiz. Good thing too because there was a pop quiz.

"Bruh, that part in the club was crazy!" Trouble dared. His lips pursed and head cocked to see if he could recall it.

"Yeah, I liked the part in Haiti! The chick Katrina was wild!" He shot back. They went back and forth about The Dark Prince movie until he pulled up to Jessie's trailer. "I'm here."

"Bet," he said and clicked over to take Jessie's incoming call.

"He here!" She said with obvious apprehension.

"He cool baby. Just take the pack," he coaxed. He listened on her end as Pablo dropped off the package. Pablo texted back that he was done and turned around to head back to Atlanta.

"This too big!" She reeled when she saw the dildo shaped package of dope.

"I know," he said and shook his head at just how tight the big girls box was. It would fit nicely under one of her rolls of fat so he picked his words carefully, not to offend. "You know how you lifted your tummy so I can get deep in that pussy?"

"Yeah!" She giggled and shook, shaking the trailer.

"Do that, then lay the pack down and lay yo tummy over it..." He said and paused while she tried it.

"It worked!" She cheered. Who would have thought the roll of flesh and fat would one day come in handy.

"Yay!" He cheered along with her. The few ounces of meth were worth tens of thousands of dollars. The product was better than the Mexican's and just as good as the White boys. It was about to go down, in more ways than one.

"You finna have to fuck me real good when I come to work," she declared.

"Shit, I'm finna fuck you real good when you come to work!" He shot back. He was looking forward to adding some pleasure to his business.

"Sup Jone," Stack greeted as he returned from the yard call. Trouble always missed weekend yard since he would be in visitation.

"Sup shawty. What I miss?" He asked since something was usually happening on the yard. His phone hadn't blown up, which meant his people didn't have any beefs.

"Shit. Err body shook after them killings," Stack relayed. First Fuck-Shit killed George on the yard, then Connor killed five in his cell. Both would been taken to the county jail and charged with murder and murders.

That had everyone subdued since shit had just gotten real. It was all good when you could bust a head or stab someone a hundred times and just get a disciplinary report. The local authorities now demanded a body in their cells for each body in their hospital or morgue. Warden Mays wanted to dig some holes on the yard to bury them there to keep down the heat. Davis had to talk her out of it but so far the scare tactic had the inmates shook.

"Yeah that shit was wild!" Trouble laughed but the vet heard through it. Something was eating him and he was there if he needed an ear to bend that wouldn't come back out the mouth.

"Good visit?" Stack asked, actually wondering if it was a bad visit that had the worry lines on his face.

"Hell yeah. Ate like a mug!" He cheered and rubbed his protruding belly. He would have left it there if up to him. It wasn't though and the next words poured out on their own. "I think my gal is fucking around tho."

"She keeping bread on yo books? Money on the phone? Yo kid straight? Money straight! And you worried about her pussy?" Stack asked. "Hold that thought until I come back."

"Ok," he said and cleared the cell so his bunk-mate could get ready to hit the shower. He saw Zay and another Rider posted up near the wall phones and went the other way. He needed some peace to sort through the fog in his mind.

He mentally set up the scales and sorted through the facts. Yes, she did keep money on his books, his kid was good, she kept his money exactly to the ledger he kept. He had more than most and shouldn't be complaining.

"Man that's some good ass pussy tho!" He moaned to himself. He had put Pablo on her to keep an eye on her but someone still had her attention. His face twisted at the thought of her and him, but he shook that off. Pablo was loyal, that's why he trusted him with the gang and his girl. "Plus, I'll kill that nigga if he do!"

"Sup Jone?" Stack asked Trouble upon his return to the cell.

"It's all good," he managed to get out. It was more possessiveness than love that kept him holding on. "Anyway, we should have that pack in a few."

"I still don't think that's a good idea shawty. It's a lot of shit that come with that cream," Stack warned.

"Yeah, bread. It's a lot of bread come with that shit. Fuck them white boys!" Trouble shot back. He wasn't the only one saying fuck those white boys.

~

"MAN FUCK THEM WHITE BOYS!" ONE EYED DINO ROARED. HE lost five of his people fucking around with Rabbit. Never mind that Rabbit paid him the rest of the money, which he now got to keep since his hitters got hit. They were stretched out on slabs at the morgue so they weren't getting their cut.

"That's fucked up!" Cupcake lamented over the losses.

"Nasty Nate was a good dude!" Honey Bun added, then added a little bit too much. "No one eat ass like Nasty Nate!"

"Well, they don't call him nasty for nothing," Dino sighed since they were now calling him the deceased. He was slightly amazed that one man ran through eight, killing five. The other three were recovering in the infirmary but weren't coming back on compound once they did.

"You think Rabbit told him they were coming? To make you look bad?" Nutty Bar offered as he rubbed Dino's feet. He had really become quite a good woman over the weeks since getting turned out. He cooked, cleaned and gave mean foot massages along with his other daily duties.

"No telling with them white hoes," he hummed and thought about it. Rabbit had reason to make him look bad since he used to rape him and all. He leaned back, whipped out and let Nutty Bar perform another of his duties while he thought.

"Either way, we gotta get some get back for our people," Honey Bun advised. This was still prison after all and shit like that can't be allowed to slide. The Bandos would look weak it they didn't do something.

"We still getting money out them," Dino added as he thought. Honey Bun was right but he had to measure his response so he wouldn't fuck up his money. Not until he found a new connect, then he could kill Rabbit once and for all. "Get five of theirs!"

"Get Chocolate, Sweet tart, M&M, Swiss roll..." Honey Bun rattled into his phone to summon the sissies. Once they departed Dino pulled his own phone and made a call.

"I already know what you're going to say!" Rabbit sighed on the line when he took the call. He knew he owed for the fiasco and would rather pay up than go to war. War cost money, not made it and he preferred to make money.

"I doubt that," Dino said and paused as Nutty Bar completed his job. It was perfect timing since he wanted Rabbit to hear the familiar grunts and groans.

"Call me back!" Rabbit snapped and clicked off. Not only did he recall the grunts and groans but the choking feeling of him way down his throat. A sharp phantom pain in his ass made him slam the phone against the wall. It shattered and his pet bunk-mate Merle scrambled to pick up the pieces.

"The fuck?" Ghost asked as he walked in a moment later and saw the shattered phone.

"This Connor shit is going to be a problem!" He advised.

"Yeah," he replied instead of the 'I told you so' on the tip of his tongue. Ghost knew they had the numbers to go up against any other faction and didn't agree with setting Connor up like that. Partly since he had never been violated. "Fuck those niggas! They want smoke, we give them smoke!"

"Yeah," Rabbit agreed as he put the old sim card in the new phone. His outburst cost him the thousand dollars that the phones were going for at the moment. Dino was ringing the line as soon as he turned it on. "Yeah."

"My bad. Had to feed my lil bitch her lunch," he laughed.

"You were saying something about that Connor thing?" He cut in before he said something else crazy. Precisely why he didn't have him on speaker, so he couldn't reveal their secret.

"Five. I need five. Five will make us even," Dino explained.

"Sheesh, that's a lot!" Rabbit said, assuming he meant ounces. Ounces of meth went for four thousand wholesale, so five equaled twenty grand.

"Five of mine died, so five of yours will make us even. Pick em, and let me know," he clarified.

"I'll give you one. That's it," Rabbit shot back. He knew he owed but also knew he had the upper hand since he had the work. Dino was spending real good with him, which meant he was eating even better. The negotiations came to a close when he hung up on the monster.

"What that one eyed cock sucking nigger want?" Ghost wanted to know.

"We're working it out..." He replied since he was the one. Ghost was a threat to his authority and had to go.

~

"HEY!" JESSIE GIGGLED LIKE A GIRL WITH A SECRET. FITTING since she was fitted with twenty thousand dollars worth of dope.

"Hey ya self sexy," he said, causing her to look around the room for someone sexy.

"Me?" She checked since she had been called lots of things in her life. None of them were sexy.

"Hell yeah," he said and undid his pants to free his erection. His dick got hard on the way over here, like it knew where he was going.

"Mmhm," she giggled and came out of her big pants and big girl panties. She lifted her tummy to produce the dope but Trouble just tossed it aside. Each ounce was worth four thousand wholesale but three to four times that amount broken down. Right now he was in search of something far more valuable. Some good pussy. Good pussy attached to a good woman is more valuable than a Bitcoin.

"This shit, is amazing!" Trouble declared as he watched himself part her plump lips and sink inside. A puddle of juice came out as he pushed in. Jessie was a big girl but couldn't take much dick. She hissed and squirmed and made faces while he pumped her plump pussy. He didn't strap up but did pull out and skeet on the floor. Then went back in and did it again, and again.

"I gotta go," he said mainly to himself since he had work to do. He had customers waiting on the product while he was up in her.

"We gonna do it again?" She pouted as she watched the dick disappear in his pants.

"We're definitely doing it again," he assured her and hit the door. There was a line outside but it didn't bother him. They could have her lips, tongue and throat, the pussy was his.

Chapter Three

"*S*up Jone, you straight?" Stack asked when Trouble returned to the cell. It was a rhetorical question since people move a different way when they're dirty.

"Hell yeah!" He said and began removing the egg shaped ounces of dope. Lil-Zay knocked on the cell door and waited for the nod. "Come on shawty."

"Dang shawty!" Zay cheered at the work. Meanwhile Stack slid out of the door to let them handle their business.

"We finna break these down. The White boys sell caps for a 'hunnid, ours go for ninety!" Trouble said of the chain gang measurement standard. The cap was actually the cap of a ChapStick tube. They measured it in it before putting it in plastic for sales. Most times it wouldn't reach that same cap full once it reached the end user. There was a middle man for each step who took their cut.

"We selling dubs too?" Zay asked since there was a healthy market for twenties. Junkies could pay for those with food items instead of cash app and PayPal.

"Fuck yeah! Dimes, nicks, whatever they got!" Trouble declared. He saw the White boys turning their noses up at the smaller sales but he wanted it all. "Take these and make sure each dorm got work. Fiddy-fiddy on the sales!"

"Hell yeah!" Zay laughed. Trouble made sure his whole

team was eating, that's why they followed him. He took the work and rushed off to carryout his duties. There was a few minutes to spare so he made a quick detour.

Zay hit his own cell and pulled out his cell phone. He quickly sent ninety dollars to the cash app set up for sales. That allowed him to pull a cap from the supply. He dumped a small amount out onto his desk and made a line. Some junkies roll a piece of paper to use as a straw but he didn't have time for all that. He leaned down and snorted the whole line up one nostril. He wasn't the only junkie in the making.

"Sup Lil-Zay," Gip asked when Zay stepped from his cell.

"What you want to be up?" He shot back in case the kid wanted to fight again. They both had been working out daily since the day they fought to a draw. There would be a next time and both planned to win. Gip wanted someone else to be denied access to the kiosk because they looked different.

"Word on the street is y'all got dubs?" He asked and looked around.

"Dang!" Zay had declared. The chain gang grapevine was in full effect. News travels at the speed of sound around here because Trouble had just put the word out.

"Hell yeah," he said since a sale was a sale. An enemy's money spends just as good as a friend's. Even better when it's on some self destructive shit like this.

"Aight, Rallo said holla at him," he said and led the way. Zay discretely touched the shank in his shirt just in case this was a setup. He followed him down to Rallo's smoke filled cell and went inside.

"Y'all niggas smoking good!" Zay proclaimed and inhaled deep enough to get a drag off the weed.

"Rollers smoke good! Drank good!" Rallo declared and held up a bottle of buck as proof. The murky liquid inside did double duty and got you drunk as well as cleaned out the bowels.

"Check," Zay nodded since he didn't care. "Y'all tryna cop some cream?"

"That Mexican shit or y'all working for the White boys?"

Rallo asked which proved why he sent for him instead of his cousin.

"Dis our shit! Riders keep a mule!" He bragged. He sounded good but gave up way too much information. The exact information Rallo was after.

"Let me see a dub. Give him that," Rallo said to Zay before turning to Gip. Gip grabbed a net bag filled with food and passed it off.

"That's twenty?" Zay squinted as he accepted the bag. It was filled with honey buns, soups and soda but he couldn't count it. He was fine when dealing with whole numbers but the fractions were a problem.

"Hell yeah," Rallo said and accepted the drug. Zay turned to leave and they twisted the meth into their next joint. The Rollers were about to roll out.

"So we're in business with the gang bangers now? First the fags, now the little nigger gang bangers," Ghost lamented to Chop.

"Could be the Mexicans?" Chop offered since he was loyal to Rabbit. At the same time he was still disloyal enough to lend an ear to the treason. The word about the Riders selling meth had now reached the White boys as well.

"No! Its not that trash!" Ghost shot back and produced the twenty dollar sample he purchased to sample. It was only half left since he sampled the other half of the sample. He was high enough to know it wasn't the mediocre Mexican dope.

"No, it's not the Mexicans!" Chop agreed the second he injected the balance into his veins.

"There's something off. Not right..." Ghost was saying until the person he was backbiting appeared. A classic, 'speak of the devil' moment if ever there was one.

"Not right about what?" Rabbit asked and looked between the two. Chop still had the needle in his arm and he assumed he meant the dope.

"That game last night. Fucking niggers taking over baseball too! What's next?" He complained. He would always have a complaint since black people were making strides in everything under the sun.

"Fucking niggers," Rabbit agreed. "Speaking of which. I need you to take this over to One Eyed Dino."

"Me?" Ghost asked curiously since he didn't usually do deliveries. In fact, he never did so this was an odd request.

"Yeah, you," he said, tossed the ounce of the dope at him and walked off.

"Want me to do it?" Chop said since he was moving a hundred miles a minute off the drug.

"Naw, I got it," he said and grabbed his knife. Rabbit could be all kumbaya with the niggers but he didn't trust them.

The White boys usually did transactions at yard but he was sent to the laundry where Dino worked. It was his assigned detail but he didn't do much work since the detail officer was one of them. Instead he used it to distribute his products through the whole prison with the clothes. A large bin came from every dorm with clothes and food items every day. Every day it went back with weed, tobacco, phones and meth.

"Un-uh, who you here to see?" A white sissy called Vanilla Latte demanded when Ghost appeared. The officer was just for show since the inmates ran the show. Dino was at his desk looking at gay porn online while the officer slept.

"Dino. Rabbit sent me," he explained. Dino heard his name and rolled his eye in that direction. He was slightly shocked to see Rabbit sent his own second in command as a sacrifice but he shouldn't be. The gang leaders were only loyal to themselves and sold their own people out any chance they got.

"Around here," Dino said and gave the nod that armed his people. They all gathered their knives to await the next nod that would poke more holes into the man than one of these net bags. The nod was slow since Dino had a question or two. "Why you?"

"Why me what? I'm a White boy!" Ghost declared and

stuck his chest out. His hand slid closer to the knife in case he had to pull it. He thought he might when the sissies surrounded him.

"Aht, aht. Pull that banger and I'ma take it from you, poke a hole in your side and fuck you in it?" Dino growled as the others came near. "You ever been fucked in your spleen white boy?"

"Oooh I have!" Vanilla Latte moaned and whined his narrow ass.

"Look it bro. I don't want no smoke. Just came to drop this off," Ghost offered as he gingerly came out with the package.

"You don't want no smoke but you came here scrapped?" Fruit Roll Up asked and popped his big lips.

"Nigga you is the smoke! You don't even know why you here do you?" Dino asked and squinted. Tried to squint, but its hard with just one eye so he opened it back.

"Yeah, you wanted five for the five uh, men, you lost. Rabbit said one. This is the one!" He said still trying to pass off the dope so he could go.

"Nah nigga. I wanted five white boys for the five Bandos I lost. He agreed to one. You that one!" Dino said with the nod that brought out the bangers. Ghost's eyes went wide when he saw the various size blades made of various materials. Vanilla Latte had a dangerous looking ice pick made from a fan. It was long enough to go completely through him.

"I don't, I mean he..." Ghost pleaded but couldn't find the right words to beg for his life. He decided to take it like a man and stuck his chest out. "Come on with it!"

"Wait!" Dino called a split second before Apple Pie split his head with a machete. A better idea spread a brilliant smile on Dino's handsome face. "Rabbit ever tell you where he knows me from? About juvie?"

"Huh? No, what?" The White boy asked, hoping it was a long story. He was relieved when the next nod lowered the knives.

"Yeah, Rabbit and I go way back. Twenty years. I used to fuck him in juvenile," Dino said and enjoyed the mixed look of disgust and horror on his face. Many gang members would be shocked to know their big homie likes ass or dick or both.

"Fuck outa here!" Ghost laughed dryly. He saw the serious look on his face and knew Dino was telling the truth. The sissies in attendance all nodded along with the facts.

"He had some fiyah head back in the day. Used to put his hands behind his back and just work his neck," Dino lied. Vanilla Latte mimicked the movement he knew so well. Even if it wasn't true. Dino had his way with Rabbit but had to fight for it each time.

"So, he's a fucking fag?" Ghost asked with a disgusted grimaces. Until he remembered he was surrounded by fucking fags. "I mean, no offense."

"None taken. You can't suck dick and be sensitive," Apple Pie reasoned. Makes sense since a dick in the booty is worse than words. Sticks and stones may break bones but that's got to be worse.

"Your boss has the best pussy on compound. I'm coming for some more, soon. If my bitch is y'all mama, that make me y'all daddy," Dino laughed and snatched the dope from his hand. Ghost was ready to die but he stepped aside and let him pass.

Dino was as smart as he was ruthless and knew he just caused Rabbit more problems. Fitting since it was Rabbit season.

Chapter Four

*S*a'id stared out the window and at the freedom that lay just beyond the fence. It was nothing more than just trees but they were free trees and that was worth everything. His lips moved along with his silent recitation of the Qur'an. A smile spread on his heart when he reached a particularly hopeful verse.

'Inna ma'al 'usri yusri' that with difficulty comes ease. Prison was definitely difficult but ease lay just beyond that fence line.

"As salaamu alaykum Sa'id," Shakur greeted with a long face. His head was big enough as it were so the long face told Sa'id something bad was behind it.

"Wa alaykum as salaam. What happened?" He asked and subconsciously held his breath. A good habit he picked up over the years, to prevent his first thought from escaping his mouth. Now he had at least a breath to think before he spoke.

"They just came and got lil Bruh," the older brother said since he didn't like the name Fuck-Shit. Even if he did earn every letter of it. Still, the whole compound knew that Rallo called the shot that killed the man. A shot that wasn't his to call since the kid told him he wanted out.

"Raheem? Who? The county?" He asked and answered as he went along. He gave his own answers so Shakur just nodded. Sa'id had plenty of time to think so when his mouth next opened he meant every syllable to follow. "If that kid gets convicted I'm going to kill Rallo with my own hands!"

"Akhi, you're on your way home! Don't mess that up for no one!" The elder brother pleaded. Sa'id turned away to look back out the window. He hoped to calm down but only made it worse when he saw the local sheriff vehicle pulling away. He couldn't make out the figure in the backseat but it could only be one person.

"He's just a kid," he said and shook his head.

"And this Rallo is a piece of shit on the highway. Just swerve around him and let the next truck run him down!" Shakur pleaded. All Sa'id could do was watch the car leave the parking lot and disappear. He said what he said and was a man of his word. After all, keeping your word is one of the things that make a male a man.

"HOW LONG I GOTTA STAY HERE?" FUCK-SHIT ASKED WHEN HE arrived at the county jail after weeks in the hole. They had been threatening to give him free world charges since killing George on the yard. He thought it was a bluff until they finally came and got him.

"Just long enough to stand trial for killing that boy," the jail guard said as they reached the cell. Most of the jail was open dorms since they didn't get many serious crimes down here. The few cells were for the worst of the worst and he had to share.

"Un-uh! Oh hell naw! That's fucking Freddy Kruger!" Fuck-Shit moaned when he saw who else was in the cell.

"Cool ain't it"! The guard laughed and shoved him inside. Fuck-Shit stumbled and landed right at Connor's feet.

"Don't hurt me bro!" He pleaded and crossed his arms to protect his face since rumor had it Connor had ate one of his victims face.

"I'm not going to hurt you bro," Connor said softly. The soft tone contradicted the raw, bruised hands he kneaded while rocking on the bunk.

Fuck-Shit slowly stood and backed against the bars of the cell. He squinted at the handsome man and didn't see a trace of the monster that beheaded and defaced five men. That dorm had been locked down for days to clean up the carnage. The killings were brutal but couldn't compare with the rumors.

"Did you really eat that man face?" Fuck-Shit needed to know. His own would probably taste like alphabet soup with all the words and letters on his face.

"No. Nor are any pieces missing and I didn't have sex with the head, I didn't..." He said debunking just the rumors he had heard. He would never be able to keep up with them all since inmates pump out rumors quicker than a Chinese factory does with bootleg Jordan's.

"You think they really finna charge us with murder?" Fuck-shit whined.

"They already did. That's why we're here," Connor explained. His family had already sent a small army of lawyers down here to represent him. None of them liked the facts of the case so they called in the big guns. An old time law vet who never lost a case. If anyone could beat these murders it would be him.

Fuck-Shit was pretty much fucked since he didn't have family. He got on the fuck shit because he had to eat. He would be stuck with a public defender who couldn't tell his ass from his elbow. Something else youngsters need to weigh in with the next lick. Rich people can literally get away with murder while poor people have to plead out to shit they really didn't do. Forced to take ten or twelve years or have a life sentenced shoved down their throats.

"Shit I'ma, I'll just say, shoot..." The kid rambled and got nowhere. He eyes suddenly went bright when he recalled something he had heard in the Friday prayer. Sa'id reminded that only in the remembrance of Allah do hearts find rest. He laid his belongings on the top bunk and headed to the small sink. He made his ablution and stretched out his prayer rug.

Connor got up and leaned against the bars to give the kid some room. Growing up in the Buckhead section of Atlanta put him in contact with plenty of Muslims so he knew what the kid was doing. He may have solely relied on the all mighty dollar but did respect the religion. The two young men from opposite sides of the track would be stuck with each other until trial. The court system wasn't jammed packed like the city so it would be months, not years.

~

"YOUR BOYFRIEND BARELY MADE IT," WARDEN MAYS lamented when her deputy walked into her office.

"Huh?" Davis asked instead of asking which one. That's one of the downsides to doing so much dirt. You never know which one will come back first. PBTP was selling pussy by the ton and she was getting rich.

"The Rallo fellow. His payments are getting slower. It may be time to cut them off? The Rollers seem to be more trouble than they're worth?" the woman wondered and watched to see where her deputy's reply came from. A quick response is from the heart or the vagina. Decisions from the brain often take a moment of contemplation. She was relieved with the pause that preceded the reply.

"True, but I wonder what those hyenas would do if we cut them completely off? The losses may be cheaper than the chaos," she reasoned. It was pretty reasonable too since the Rollers were the cause of most of the drama in the facility.

"What if they changed leaders?" the warden wondered.

"Might help. Might not since Rallo will just call the shots from wherever we ship him," Davis replied.

"From out back?" Mays asked. She had been at the prison since it opened and no one ever did anything from out back. That's what they called the cemetery behind the prison. Most inmates out back died of old age or illness. Others were killed in the line of duty, others were sent by the administration.

"I'll keep an eye on his second in command and let you know if that helps or hurts,". the deputy warden replied. She summoned her snitch in the dorm with Mac town on put him to work.

Chapter Five

"*Mmph!*" Malaysia groaned and instantly regretted the outburst.

"What?" Trouble asked from across the table as he bounced their baby on his lap.

"Huh?" She asked since the answer was the glob of come coming back down. Pablo had just skeeted it up into her this morning before she got on the road. Having him spend the night allowed her to bring the baby to see his daddy.

"You said, never mind," he began than abandoned. He remembered what Stack told him and kept it to himself. His son was clean and healthy and the numbers were right so he had to overlook the obvious. What wasn't obvious was how badly she didn't want to be here.

"I'ma give granny some money. If that's alright with you," she advised.

"Of course," he agreed since he had always gave back to the woman who raised him. She still had a house full of kids to take care of just like she took care of him.

"Trouble, I got something to tell you," she blurted and held her head in shame. Trouble twisted his lips and contemplated for a moment to see if he really wanted to hear it or not.

"What?" He heard himself ask before making his decision. It was out so he let it be.

"Rallo the one robbed our house," she said with her head still down. It slowly lifted when he didn't reply. Silence is torture for a guilty person and as such she talked some more. "He the one gave Reecie a ride out to Marrietta. He did drop her at the Wendy's, but followed her to see where we stayed."

"Mmm," Trouble hummed with a nod. He remained quiet to keep her talking.

"I ain't say nothing at first since you just had got yo time," she pouted.

"Mmhm," he hummed and waited for more. The truth would be mixed in there somewhere like a puzzle. He had all of the end pieces, now it was time to fill it in.

"Then, I was finna tell you when you got here but, when you called you was like 'guess who here?'. I was like 'who?'. You said 'Rallo' and y'all was in the same dorm! I was like un-uh!" She explained.

"Hmm," he hummed to see if there was more.

"And they said you can come home early if you stay out of trouble so, I ain't say nothing," she sighed.

"So, why you telling me now?" He had to wonder. Even he knew his blood should be boiling at the revelation. It now explained the look on Rallo's face when he saw him in the dorm. That look that comes when the opps catch you lacking.

"Huh?" She answered since he wouldn't like the real answer. She wouldn't mind if he stayed the full ten years so she could be with Pablo.

"Can I get another pop?" He asked and nuzzled his son.

"Sure. Grape I know. You love you some grape!" She said happily and hopped up to retrieve it.

Trouble usually joined half the men in the visitation room in watching her fat ass in motion whenever it was in motion. In the right pants it had more drama than a Broadway play. It suddenly lost it's appeal. He just needed her to take care of his son and money. His heart was no longer invested in her.

They hugged like cousins should hug when it was time to go. He saved the kisses for little Trevor's chubby cheeks. The baby cooed and giggled before he handed him back to his mother. He gave a longing look knowing any time could be the last time for a while. Neither looked back as they separated and went back to their lives.

Malaysia looked around for her car and shook her head when she saw Pablo's since he drove her down. He killed two birds with one stone since he had to drop off the work to Jessie. He was now a partner in the business since Malaysia had went on a shopping spree with the re-up money. She was still spending recklessly since half was hers and all. All she would have to do was stop spending and stack up his half before he came home. No problem.

"How's the brother?" Pablo asked sincerely as she buckled the baby into the car seat. He may have been smashing his lady but had genuine love for the man.

"He good. I hope he don't get in no trouble tho," she moaned, even though she deliberately just set some trouble in motion. Him killing Rallo would actually kill two birds with one stone as well. First because he needed to pay for violating them. Little did she know JJ was paying daily and nightly with his larynx and rectum. Then, if he did kill Rallo he would stay here and she could stay with Pablo.

"What?" Pablo asked of the devious smirk the dastardly plan put on her face.

"Huh? Nothing. You handled yo biz?" She asked to change the subject from her.

"Yeeeeaaah," he drew out with a grimace. He understood taking one for the team but couldn't imagine having sex with big Jessie. He also didn't understand how Malaysia talked him into paying for the re-up and becoming a third in the business.

"Well, let me thank you properly for taking care of us and driving us," she said as she went for his zipper. She wriggle his flaccid dick free and leaned over into his lap. The blow job answered his last question. She used what she had, to get what she wanted.

∾

Fate is a motherfucker and as such, Rallo was the first face Trouble faced when he returned to the dorm. He felt a slight rumble in his soul but managed to subdue it before he acted upon it. Stack always told him this was chess, not checkers. Ain't no sudden moves in chess.

"Sup cuz!" Trouble cheered and threw out his palm.

"Sup?" Rallo greeted back after making sure his hand was empty. "How the fam?"

"Err body good. Granny good," he said since he knew the man didn't call the woman who raised him. He was making good money but didn't send her a coin. Black hearts do black hearted shit so it just wasn't in him. Once a heart goes dead you may as well throw the whole body away.

"Yeah, I talked to, mmhm, un-uh," he said but the whole lie couldn't get through his throat. He did pay Reecie for pussy pics but other than that didn't have much contact with the family.

"Shit, let's smoke one! I'll grab a stick and fall through," Trouble announced. He didn't await an answer since addicts don't turn down free drugs. He headed to his cell to come out of his visit clothes and grab some weed.

"What you got going on Jone?" Stack laughed when he came in. He seen Trouble grinning with Rallo and knew something was up. They were usually cordial, never grinning.

"Shit. Finna rock this baby to sleep," he replied. Stack nodded on his way out since that's a chess move.

Trouble changed, grabbed a stick of weed and headed over to Rallo's cell. It was full of Rollers as usual since they couldn't stand on their own. When a man becomes a man he enjoys his own company more than a bunch of people around all the time.

"Sup cuz!" Trouble greeted and tapped on the door.

"Y'all 'scuse us," Rallo said to dismiss his crew.

"You need me to stay?" Gip asked but only because he still didn't believe shit stank. Trouble beat him up last time but he had done plenty of pushups since then. He was ready.

"Naw, cuz you might miss store call again and you owe me some bread!" Rallo laughed.

"He gone be alright," Trouble said as the Rollers left the cell. The Riders were all watching the cell to watch their leaders back so the two groups just watched each other.

"Check this shit out!" Rallo said and passed his phone. A plump vagina was being spread with two fingers on the screen. "Shit fat huh!"

"Hell yeah!" He had to admit since it was pretty fat and all. He had no idea it belonged to his little cousin Reecie though. He pulled a lighter and lit the weed and took a few pulls.

The two made small talk as they smoked but Trouble was here on a reconnaissance mission. His eyes discretely ran around the room while they gossiped about what was happening around the chain gang and their old hood.

'Could kill you right now' Trouble thought when spotted a large knife on the bed. It was close enough to grab and shove into his neck while he took a long, greedy pull off the weed. *'Too easy'*.

Rallo needed a slow death for his treachery and betrayal.

"So, you, heard, about that nigga, Fuck-Shit? They finna free, world, him," Rallo asked between sips of air and pulling on the joint. He was trying to suck all he could out of the free weed.

"Yeah, that's fucked up. I thought he was Muslim now?" Trouble asked. Rumors of a beef were slowly brewing like tea bags in a gallon jug, in the Arizona sun.

"He was tryna be. I made him put in some work first tho," he bragged and Trouble nodded. That could come back to haunt him but he still glanced around in search of other ways to hurt him.

"The Muslims might want some smoke behind that?" Trouble dared. He almost missed the syringe on the desk as scanned it.

"Man fuck them folks! Rollers with the shit!" He cheered and attempted to pass the wet roach back.

"I'm good cuz," he declined and stood since he had what he needed. First the gang of junkie kids would get slaughtered if they went against the Muslims. If they didn't get him that syringe would. He would make sure to funnel plenty of meth his way to keep it full. "Oh, here."

"What's this for?" Rallo asked after taking the drugs from his palm.

"We fam shawty," Trouble said sincerely. Chess, not checkers.

Chapter Six

" *H*ightower, pack it up!" The officer announced and set off series of announcements. One of the strange phenomenon's of prison life is inmates love to make announcements. It was loud enough through the loud speaker but men echoed the call anyway.

"Say Stack! They calling you!" A man announced as he knocked on the frame of Stack's door.

"I hear them Jone," he said and headed out to see what the officer wanted.

"Aye Stack, the police calling you," Trouble joked as he walked out.

"Ion know what they mean, pack it up? I ain't finna move no where!" He insisted as he went to see what was going on.

Prison is extremely transient, and you can switch cells, dorms or even facilities without reason. Like someone playing a game of chess, moving real people as pieces. Sometimes its necessary to balance the gang bangers. Other times vets like Stack were moved to problem dorms to restore order since his presence alone cut down on some of the fuck shit. Sometimes all people need is their ass whipped one good time to make them see things in a different light.

"Pack it up Hightower," the officer repeated through the intercom.

"To go where?" He dared since he wouldn't go just anywhere. He heard the response and staggered back to his cell like a drunk.

"Fuck wrong with you Jone?" Trouble asked an squinted to see if he could see.

"I um, I'm..." Stack stammered as if having trouble getting the words out. He cleared his throat and tried again. "I got a teletype. I'm going home."

"Shit pack it up then nigga!" Trouble cheered and jumped up to help him.

"Ain't shit to pack," he said and grabbed the bible his mom sent as well as his thick photo album. The rest was prison shit and needed to stay in prison. "Give this food to dad upstairs. The phone go to Pittsburgh..."

"OK, un-uh, OK," Trouble repeated as he took the instructions. The world traveled throughout the dorm which exploded in applause when Stack stepped from his cell. After thirty years the chain gang legend was going home.

"Remember what I said," Stack reminded as Trouble walked him to intake. It also served as outtake but more men came than went so it was called intake.

"Which one?" He laughed since the vet had taught him everything. He learned how to stack his bread and carry himself like a G in the few months they had been together in the same cell.

"All dat shit shawty!" He laughed with him and embraced him like a son. He saw another smiling face coming to see him off and turned.

"Alhamdulillah!" Sa'id chanted for his partner and dapped him up.

"You next shawty!" Stack assured him as they embraced.

"In sha Allah. I'll see you in that city in a few," he agreed. "Same number?"

"Same number," he nodded and turned to leave. Stack Cascade processed out and left the building. Just in time to miss the new arrivals.

~

New arrivals day is usually a big day for everyone involved. It was a chance for Sergeant Quick and his CERT team to flex some muscle and beat someone up. A chance for Sergeant Pike to update her roster of gang bangers. A fresh flock of junkies for the wardens to eat off. A chance for gangs to recruit new members.

Some faces were new since this was their first bid. Of them, prison would prove horrible enough to deter from future crimes. Others were frequent flyers who made reservations to return over and over. Prison wasn't so bad for them so they didn't mind coming back. Recidivism should actually be labeled as a mental illness because those motherfuckers are crazy. Got to be to keep coming back to this shit.

Dino especially loved it because it meant new meat. Literally, new cheeks for the notorious booty bandit to exploit.

"Oh yeah. Hell yeah, hell yeah!" Dino cheered from the window. He had a raging erection just from the bus pulling in. He just hoped it was full of white boys and two thousand babies. Young white boys were his own little reparations for slavery. He took out four hundred years of oppression by oppressing them.

He usually jacked off while watching the new arrivals arrive but now he had Nutty Bar at his beck and call. He was like a fee-fee with feet who came running when called. He was knelt below as Dino one eyed the new arrivals filing off the bus.

"Mmm, white boys, two thousand babies, another white boy, what's that a Korean? Chinese? Two thousand baby..." All that excitement proved to much for Dino. He grunted and nearly knocked poor Nutty Bar over.

"Let me see!" He said as he scrambled to his feet. A few inmates enjoyed watching the new inmates getting punked fresh off the bus like they were. "Ooh I know him! Him a Rider!"

"A dick rider?" Dino asked hopefully as he peered his one eye at the young man getting yelled at by Sergeant Quick and his crew. He was a pretty, black boy just like he liked.

"Prolly," Nutty Bar guessed since he was a two thousand baby. "They call him Bama."

∽

"SAY SHAWTY, GUESS WHO HERE!" LIL-ZAY ASKED EXCITEDLY as he rushed into Trouble's half empty cell. It seems like three times the normal size with just one person in it. Despite it being the size of the average apartment bathroom.

"Nuh-uh," Trouble declined. He had been a street nigga his whole life. All he knew was street niggas, so the list to guess from could take months.

"Huh?" Zay asked since subtleties got by him. Stack had taught him how to speak without speaking but those lessons were wasted on the youngster.

A leader can only lead people who want to go where they are trying to take them. Lil-Zay's plans were to hit those same streets that sent him to prison. He was trying his best to do his whole ten, while Trouble was trying in the opposite direction. Lil-Zay bucked details and stayed high. Trouble was in GED class and scrubbed pots in the kitchen in between his drug dealing.

"Just tell me who, so I can get back to my social studies," Trouble said. It was easier than trying to explain what he meant.

"How that shit 'sposed to help us slang dope tho?" The young man asked. It was as confusing to him as some of these dates Trouble had to memorize for his test. Lil-Zay was a dope boy and that's all he aspired to be. Social studies may not help the average businessman run his business but a GED would.

Trouble on the other hand had other aspirations. Being in prison put him in close contact with criminals from all walks of life. They may have had different upbringings and different crimes but there is only one chain gang. The common denominator between him and them were the drugs. He came from the bottom so he was used to seeing junkies. Seeing people throw everything away to get high was harder to figure out than the math section of the test.

He now had bigger plans than the ones that put him in here. If junkies could grow legit businesses, so could he. So would he. At the rate he was hustling he would have at least a half a million upon early release. More than enough to start a new life with his new chick. He didn't know who she was just yet but knew it wasn't Malaysia. She could be in the country of Malaysia for he knew, but it wasn't her.

Trouble was intuitive enough to know she was fucking someone. Stack left him with a jewel so he appreciated her for holding him down. She was still his cousin though and that nagged the back of his mind like wondering if you cut the stove off before you left home. She had seduced him one night that turned into years.

The way his loyalty was set up it never crossed his mind that Pablo would cross him. He was a nerdy wannabe who wanted to be like Trouble. His knack for numbers made him a nice addition to the Riders. He even had a spot for him when he went legit.

"You ain't even listening to me shawty!" Lil-Zay complained and waved his hand in front of Trouble's face to bring him back to the present.

"Huh? What?" Trouble asked since he did miss what he said.

"I said that nigga Bama is here! Here at D-block!"

~

"AFFILIATION?" SERGEANT PIKE ASKED WITHOUT EVEN looking up. She had a talent for picking the right gang and set with a glance. It was part art but they made it easy as well. Kids today are dick riders by nature and all emulate each other. Sadly its usually for some dumb shit. One day some cool person is going to make school, jobs, marriage and family popular and black people can reach the heights meant for them.

"Roller," Bama said causing her to snap her face up from her screen. She frowned at the clear Riders ink and wondered what he was doing.

43

"Are you trying to get killed? They will kill you know?" She warned since false claiming will certainly get you killed. Little did she know she was talking to a dead man anyway so he played a long shot.

"Naw, not really," he said and left it at that. There was explaining that needed to be done but not to her.

"Well, I'm still noting you got Riders ink. You can do what you want to do," she huffed. She really didn't like people playing with her and wasting her time. "Hope yo ass can fight. Next!"

"Next man," Bama said as he left her office. The Mexican looked up and tilted his head as if he didn't understand.

"No hablo?" He offered Bama and looked over at the officer for clarity.

"You-a, go-a, next-a," the guard said since all you have to do is add an 'a' to the end of a word to make it Spanish. An 'I' does the same for Chinese. The small man was the same height when he stood from the chair. He shuffled into the office like a old man and looked helplessly at the sergeant.

"Cut the shit Fitz! I know who you are!" Pike laughed. The notorious Mexican had been bouncing around the system leaving a trail of bodies in his wake for twenty years. "Now, if you want to get out of here and deported back to Mexico all you need to do is, not do what you been doing!"

"I want nothing but to go home," he offered contritely. He had been a big methamphetamine dealer on the streets and an even bigger one behind the wall. A neighbor's kid snitched on him about a murder twenty years ago and cost him his freedom. A neighbor's kid called Rabbit.

Chapter Seven

"*W*hat?" Rabbit asked when he caught Ghost doing it again. Things had been strange ever since he came back from the delivery he wasn't supposed to come back from. Dino told Rabbit he charged it to the game and let it go. Still, Ghost was distant and brooding. Rabbit didn't think Dino would have revealed the hit since they were getting good money together. Enough money for both to pause their plans to murder each other.

"What, what?" Ghost asked since he wasn't sure which what he was asking about.

"You keep looking at me. Then, when I speak, you're looking right in my mouth? Like right now!" He said since Ghost was doing it right now.

"Oh. Nothing," he shrugged and turned away. The what, was he was having problems taking orders out the same mouth Dino put his dick in. He recalled the vivid mouth fucking details Dino provided of he and Rabbit in juvie. It was highly embellished but enough truth to ring true. This is how the devils do. They tell one truth and add ninety nine lies with it. The soul will pick up on the truth and accept the lies that come with it.

"OK, we just got...you're doing it again!" Rabbit fussed

when Ghost's gaze went right back into his mouth the moment he opened it.

"My bad," he said and just looked at the ground instead.

"Anyway, we just got a shipment in and orders are half what they should be. Those niggers are getting a toehold into our mountain!" He grumbled. As he should because the mountain he spoke of was a mountain of money.

"Let's take their black asses to war!" Chop Suggested as he and Ghost agreed upon during the secret meetings they held. He would be the man next to the man when Ghost launched his coup de gras.

"We can't sell shit if the camp is on lock-down dumb ass!" Rabbit fussed. He had the best dope and solid connect so patience was their best play. JC opened his mouth to put him on blast about being raped but a quick look from Ghost shut it down. It wasn't quick enough and Rabbit saw it. He was just too smart to mention it at the moment.

"He's right. He's the boss," Ghost reminded as the officer called for yard call. "Y'all go ahead. Ghost and I will catch up."

"White power!" JC and Chop offered and turned away to exit the dorm.

'He probably wants to suck me off' Ghost entertained in his mind. *'I'll let him but I'm still taking over.'*

"Listen, it's no time to screw up. I'm on my way out the door and you're next in line. The movement, the mule, the entire operation is yours!" Rabbit stressed. He could see the greed and power light the back of his eyes like a cat at night.

"The wh,wh, whole thing? The m,m,movement?" He stuttered, star struck by the idea. Most side kicks want to be the man and here was his chance. Instead of killing him he would just wait him out. He kinda wanted some head but that wasn't on the table.

"The whole movement. Now let's hit this yard!" Rabbit said and led the way. He stifled a smirk at how easy it was to manipulate people. Con men can only con greedy people and Ghost was greedy for power. Especially white power.

～

THE NEW ARRIVALS WENT THROUGH THE NEW ARRIVAL DRILL and were giving clothing and assigned to a dorm. They had just enough time to put their belongings away before yard call was called. Bama ignored the glares from both the Riders and Rollers as he walked through the dorm. The Rollers wanted to bust him since he was a Rider and the Riders wanted to bust him for being a snitch.

Rollo and Trouble had both sent word not to touch him, yet. Until then he had to deal with the daggers being shot from every angle. Yard was called and he fell to the back of the line so no one could stab him in his back with one of those daggers. Bama had a fresh twenty year sentence and knew he wouldn't make it twenty minutes if he didn't think quickly. The long bus ride gave him the chance to think long and hard so he had a solution by the time he reached D-block. He could die trying but would definitely die if he didn't.

"There go that fuck nigga now!" Lil-Zay fumed when Bama stepped out onto the yard. All eyes from every faction was on him as he squinted in the bright sunlight. Word travels quickly in prison so he had nowhere to run.

"Chill shawty..." Trouble advised. He guessed correctly that he was being tested. If his gang hit the snitch it would fall on him. Zay nodded but he had no chill in him. What he did have was a healthy dose of methamphetamine coursing through his system, telling him the exact opposite. He clutched the banger as he watched Bama head directly towards him.

Bama lifted his chin defiantly as he approached the mob of Riders ready to ride on him. A slight smirk lifted the corner of his lip which even pissed Trouble off now. He was ready to throw chill out the window and stab the man himself. Bama didn't plan to die today so he made a last second detour and headed straight for Rallo and his Rollers.

"What the fuck you wanted to talk to me about?" Rallo grimaced. Bama had made sure to put the word out the second he touched the compound to put his plan in motion.

"Cuz, the way I sees it, we allies! Yeah, I told on them niggas but that helps you!" he offered. "Y'all beefing so what better way to stick it to them than to take me in?"

"Rollers don't rock with no police!" Rallo huffed. It sounded good but half his crew had testified against co-defendants. The other half would testify against Jehovah right now if it would set them free.

"I'll pay!" he offered and wiped the snarl from Rallo's face.

"Let me holla at shawty y'all," he told the crew and pulled Bama aside to work the side deal. He was developing quite the meth habit and needed additional income to support it.

"I'm sitting on a lil something. Put me down with you and I'll break you off each month," Bama offered. If it didn't work at least he could afford a decent burial. Far more dignified than the weed covered lot Nasty Nate and other indigent inmates were buried in out back. The prison grave yard had razor wire around it to just to add a little insult to injury.

"That's what's up. But shawty, miss a payment..." Rallo warned and shook his head. He raised a hand to summon his cousin who was busy staring down his throat while they spoke.

"Fuck that fuck nigga want shawty?" Zay growled.

"I'm finna see," Trouble said and took the banger. Zay wanted to follow but Trouble waved him off. Bama would get what he earned but it wouldn't be out here in front of the world to see. The cameras pointing down at the yard were what got Fuck-Shit a murder charge. Trouble was smarter than that, this was chess and Bama just pushed a pawn. It was his move now.

"Look shawty, I know you and the homie here had beef on the 'screets, but he a Rider now," Rallo said like he said what he said. They both waited for Trouble's reply but they had to wait for him to finish laughing first. It was a good tummy hurting, knee slapping guffaw that made even Bama smile. A few full minutes later Trouble said what he had to say.

"OK, first of all, y'all can have the fuck nigga, snitch nigga, dick in the booty nigga..." he relayed. That too took a few minutes to unleash all the different kinds of insults he had on tap. Then got down to the meat and potatoes of the meal. "He still gotta shoot a one with me, then Lil-Zay."

"Bet that!" both Rallo and Bama eagerly agreed. Bama thought he could whoop them both anyway and Rallo just liked to watch people fight.

"We gotta bless him first tho," Rallo said since he still needed to be jumped into the gang.

"But, I thought..." Bama whined. He thought buying his way in meant bypassing the beat down. To make matters worse Trouble cracked a smile at the beating he hoped to escape. Bama smiled too since he still had a mental beating of his own for Trouble. "Oh OK. Can I holla at bruh for a second?"

"Make it quick!" Rallo barked and stepped off to give them space. His head nodded in satisfaction since Bama asked for permission.

"We really finna take this fuck nigga?" Mac Town whined to Rallo when he returned. He may like to get head from sissies but drew the line at snitches. It must have been an invisible line because a dick in the mouth has to be just as distasteful. Pun intended of course but homos are better than snitches. You don't have to deal with the sissies if you don't want to, but the snitches affect everyone.

"For a quick minute. Eat up the nigga bread and then sell his ass to Dino like the other one," Rallo laughed. But first we finna beat him in. Go tell the cops not to call a code, we just blessing a nigga."

"Check," he said and rushed to do just that. Most of the officers were either working with the gangs or didn't care so he gave a heads up while Bama and Trouble began to talk.

"I'm just curious, as to what the fuck you want to speak to me about?" Trouble asked looking like it hurt to even think about. The knife in his pants seemed to throb to remind him of its presence.

"Oh just wanna to tell you how I caught this case," he said with a satisfied smirk at what he had to say. Trouble twisted his lips and listened. "Yeah you got me back real good putting yo lil bitch on me!"

"The fuck you 'talmbout?" he grimaced and listened even more intently.

"Malaysia. You sent the bitch at me. You did, don't lie! She put the cops on me in the morning but I fucked her real good the night before. Yeah I seent yo name tatted by her pussy. I skeeted on that shit! Fucked her in her mouth, ass, err thing."

Trouble just blinked in disbelief even he had to believe it since she got the tattoo after she stopped dancing. Bama described the minute scar left by the C-section as well as the tight pussy with the thin strip of hair leading to it. No question he was telling the truth. The knife throbbed some more as if begging to be shoved into his neck. He was still blinking as Bama walked away to the beating he had waiting.

"What? What he say?" Zay asked when he returned. Trouble was too troubled to talk. He was ready to for the weekend so he could see Malaysia face to face. Anything could, and would come out of her mouth but her eyes didn't lie. All he needed to do was look into her eyes.

Chapter Eight

"*I*s that Trouble!" Reecie cheered when Malaysia's eyes lit up at the name on her screen. She was pregnant again by someone which gave her a break from the club. Also gave Malaysia a free babysitter as well. "Tell him I said hey!"

"Reecie said hey," Malaysia complied when she took the call that lit up her face.

"She must think it's yo baby daddy huh?" Pablo guessed correctly. He was just as gone off the P as she was off the D, and now had a problem with her and Trouble's relationship.

"Mmhm," she hummed and excused herself to her bedroom so they could talk freely and dirty.

"Miss me?" He dared but knew the answer.

"You know I do! You miss me?" She asked back even though she knew the answer as well. This may have started off as an itch that needed scratching but they were now both in love.

"Good, cuz I'm outside," Pablo smiled through the line. Malaysia popped up and rushed to her bedroom window to see for herself.

"Boy!" She giggled and gushed. She slipped her panties off in case he wanted to play in her pussy before he left.

"I told ole boy I would drop off his dough," he explained

since he was holding some money for Trouble. He was now referred to as 'ole boy' instead of his name. He separated the meth money from the money he made with the wardens but still sent some to his baby mama to hold and stack. He decided to spread a little out a little so not to keep all his eggs in one basket.

"Hmp!" She huffed since her plan to cause trouble for Trouble had yet to bare fruit. She expected him to kill Rallo by now so she wouldn't have to keep making the two hour journey each Saturday and Sunday. "Guess I'll be on the road tomorrow!"

"I'll ride with you. Gotta meet big girl again," he offered as she made her way through the living room.

"Ooh I wanna go!" Reecie pleaded when she saw her heading to the door.

"Girl I ain't going nowhere! Dang!" She fussed on her way out. Reecie jumped up and peeped out the window and watched her get into the passenger seat of Pablo's new Benz.

"Huh?" She wondered when Malaysia leaned over to kiss him. Her head tilted curiously as she kept a bead on the couple.

"Dang!" Malaysia grimaced at the fresh bank stacks of cash. Pablo was smart enough to know how to launder the dirty money into clean cash. One of the reasons he was so valuable to Trouble.

"I know right! This meth shit be booming!" he said, shaking his head.

"It do be!" She agreed and drifted away to think about what to buy with her half of the money. Even though she had spent well into his half but there was still plenty of time to put it back.

"Can I come back when I'm done?" He asked and reached between her legs to make his case.

"Ssss, my lil cousin here. She ssss, talk to mmmm, much," she moaned and got all slick and slippery on his fingers.

"So, what we, gone, do about... This?" He asked as he extracted his erection.

"Ion know?" Malaysia pouted but licked her lips. She

knew just what to do with it and leaned down to do it. She gave the throbbing head a kiss and lick before easing him into her hot mouth.

"Nuh-uh?" Reecie asked as she watched from the window. She had sucked enough dick in cars to know what she saw but didn't quite believe her eyes. She shot a glance at the babies sleeping peacefully before easing out to mind their business.

Pablo had his eyes shut too tightly to see Reecie as she crept up to the car. He was lucky she wasn't an opp because she was able to get right up on the car. She saw for herself what was really going on in the front seat. Not only was Malaysia sucking the dick, she was sucking it well.

"A'ight now!" Pablo warned since Malaysia was one of those 'don't come in my mouth' chicks. Strange creatures really since you can't really suck the dick, lick the dick, tug on the dick, and not expect what comes out the dick not to come out the dick. The only prevention is not to put the dick in the mouth in the first place. It's just a really weird contradiction that needs to stop.

Malaysia heard him and kept right on doing what she had been doing to get him there. This wouldn't be the first time but those other times she pulled away and watched him explode as she stroked him with her hand. This time she didn't budge.

"Fuck!" Pablo shouted and squirmed as he ejected on her tongue and tonsils.

"Mmhm," she urged and clamped down to take it all. She didn't move until his feet stopped shifting under them and the convulsions came to an end. "See, I ain't never did that before with ole boy."

"He still got something from you I don't," he said once he got his breathing right again.

"You for real?" She asked again since she wasn't sure if he was serious the last time they spoke about it. She wanted to do anything for him but wasn't sure how she could pull it off. He twisted his lips in reply. She let out sigh and climbed on top of him. His dick had began to deflate but she cured that ailment by rubbing it against her slippery lips.

"Fuck," he grunted when she squeezed him inside and slowly began to sink south.

'Ooooh!' Reecie gushed silently from the side. She could hardly believe what she was seeing so she pulled her phone to capture it.

"Dang boy!" Malaysia moaned but it was she doing the work. She gently rocked and wiggled while Pablo held her curvy hips. He guided her up and down until his toes began to tingle once more. They had slipped up the first time the fucked since it had been spontaneous but had practiced safe sex since then, until now.

"Finna come," he whispered, giving her a chance to change her mind. It bothered him that she had a child by Trouble while he had none. The warning went ignored again and she kept right on rocking, right on wiggling.

"Come on, then!" She said and gave a mighty squeeze. That did the trick and caused him to moan and squirm once more.

"Fuck!" Pablo grunted and groaned. He had a full night ahead of him but really just wanted a nap right now.

"Nuh-uh! Go handle your business!" Malaysia laughed and shook his eyes open. The combination of weed and pussy works better than a sedative.

"Yeah. I'll be through to get you in the morning," he sighed as she climbed off. He caught movement in the corner of his eye and turned to see Reecie scurrying away.

"Be on time so Ion have to hear ole boy mouth," she said and leaned in for a kiss. He forgot about just busting a nut in that same mouth and twirled his tongue around inside it.

"Go on now before I hit it again!" He warned. Malaysia wouldn't mind but got out to let him handle her business. She went back inside and found Reecie right where she left her. The movie was still playing so she got comfortable on the sofa.

"Girl what you sitting upside down for?" Reecie reeled.

"Oh, nothing..."

～

"HEY," BOTH TROUBLE AND MALAYSIA GREETED DRYLY AS they came face to face in the visitation room. It was a good thing they didn't kiss with those dry mouths. It would have rubbed the skin off each other's lips like sandpaper.

"Sup lil man!" Trouble gushed at his happy son. The baby smiled and kicked to say the words he hadn't learned yet. Trouble focused on him to avoid the ugly truth in her eyes. She avoided the same by rushing to the vending machines to rack up on his favorite foods. A short time ago she loved this task. Now it was just as tedious as the long ride down here had been before Pablo began driving her. It was good little Trevor couldn't speak just yet since he witnessed mommy lean her head over into uncle Pablo's lap twice on the trip down.

"Here you go," Malaysia said as she placed the hot food and cold drink on the table. The rest went under her chair to be heated on demand for the rest of the day. She was just as nice as always but the word 'baby' was noticeably absent. As well her piercing gaze. Today she looked everywhere but in his eyes.

"You'll never guess who's here?" Trouble offered, but didn't look up.

"Oooh they got you talking all proper!" Malaysia laughed at his improved speech. Just a small proof that he couldn't take her where he was trying to go anyway. "Who!"

"Bama good snitching ass," he growled. This time he did look up and so did she. The shared animosity for the man masked the other truth yet to be told.

"Good! Y'all need to detonate his ass!" she fumed. Part was for Bama snitching but just as much was for him taking the pussy. She was mad at him too for not taking the bait about Rallo. She hoped he would have killed him and wouldn't have to come down for a while.

"In time," he said and watched for her reaction. Her jaw clenched like it does when she gets angry so he knew she was. Why, was what he didn't know yet. "What them accounts saying?"

"They straight," she said and laid out what should have been in each account by now. They had already surpassed the hundred grand they lost, on paper anyway. In truth there was just over thirty thousand put away. There was still a few years before he could come home. Plenty of time to put his half back. On paper that is.

"You seen Pablo?" he asked and caught her off guard, causing her to choke on her soda. Pablo had said he hadn't seen her so he wanted to see if they matched up.

"Mph, excuse me!" she said and cleaned up the soda. "Naw, not since he dropped that last money off. I be in the house. Reecie been keeping me company."

"Oh," he sighed and wondered why she was lying. He wouldn't keep asking the man to babysit his woman. Especially now that he saw the deceit in her eyes. Stack was at home living his best life but his words stayed there with him. As long as she was holding him down he couldn't trip what she did with her pussy.

Words flowed back and forth across the table for the rest of the visit but luckily there wouldn't be a test since neither paid particular attention to the other. They didn't bother to hug when it came time to leave. He passed the baby back and turned on his heels to leave. She headed out and met Pablo in the parking lot for the ride back to the city.

Trouble had the feeling he wouldn't see her next week and he was right. He had no idea just how right he was.

Chapter Nine

"*N*ew meat!" A man called as the new arrivals entered the dorm. Every one took notice for one reason or another. Especially those with an empty bunk in their cell since that meant one of these dudes was moving in with them.

"Please, please, please," a gay guy pleaded to whoever he would plead such a thing to when he saw a sissy in the bunch. It was fate not his prayer that led the girly guy to his cell. "Yes! Thank you!"

"Bet not be the white boy," Lil-Zay growled as two men headed towards Trouble's cell. Trouble looked at the square black guy who looked up at the cell number above his door and went in. He and his crew were right behind him.

"Sup my nigga!" Trouble snarled, surrounded by Lil-Zay and the other Riders in the dorm. The show of force was meant to intimidate the new man they put in Trouble's cell. He had enjoyed the private suite for a couple of days but now had a roommate.

"Ion want no smoke!" The man said and raised his hand in surrender. There wasn't a trace a of fear in his eyes so Trouble let off the gas a little. "I'm just trying to do my time and go home. This where they put me."

"Where you from?" Trouble asked, hearing the familiar timbre even without the 'shawty shawty'.

"Atlanta," he said and extended his hand. Trouble recognized it from the etiquettes of where he was trying to go. He took the hand and dismissed his troops.

"Y'all go 'head. He good," he said as they shook. He waited until they cleared before offering, "I'm Trevor but everyone around here calls me Trouble."

"Nice to meet you Trevor, trouble. I'm Darius," he replied and returned to the task of putting his belongings away according to the diagram.

"What they got you on?" Trouble asked even though it wasn't proper to ask. He knew the square didn't abide by the laws of the chain gang since he was so green. He obviously wasn't in here for thuggjng so he needed to know it wasn't for messing with kids.

"Taxes! My partner screwed me and they give me a year!" He fussed. Trouble nodded along with him but planned to look him up when he got his phone out for the day.

"Well, you can do a year standing on your head. Just play by the rules. Look but don't see. See, but don't say..." He said and broke down the laws of the land. By the next chow call he had felt him out enough to trust him.

"Here, call your people," he said and handed him the cell phone just like Stack had done him.

"Wow!" Darius cheered with his eyes lighting up. Trouble gave him some space to let him speak to his family.

"What that square ass nigga 'talmbout?" Lil-Zay demanded when Trouble came out.

"Square shit. He cool," Trouble informed. He was more than cool in his eyes though. Hearing about the houses, cars and trips had broadened his horizons. Trouble wanted to be just like him.

~

"OOH LALA!" DINO MOANED AS THE NEW ARRIVALS SPREAD

out looking for their new homes. Five two-thousand babies had him rock hard and Nutty Bar thirty eight hot.

"You act like you ain't got a bitch!" Nutty Bar fussed with a hand on his hip. Dino smiled and gave himself a mental pat on his own back. When he turned them out they where turned way out. Dude was a whole woman now with jealousy and sass to prove it.

"Chill lil mama. Just a lil something to add to our family," he explained and gave him a kiss. One of the young boys smiled at the display and they had found their man, or whatever.

The White boys recruited the two white boys that came in right away. There was still an internal beef within their ranks but it hadn't reached the rank and file yet. The Rollers swooped in corralled the one left. They jumped him into the gang before he could even put his stuff away. Prison is full of predators and prey. He decided to be a predator so he wouldn't get preyed upon.

Dino picked up the last one and began slowly grooming him to be a girl. The teen gladly accepted the weed, food and friendship offered. He would learn the hard way that nothing in life is free, and even less in the chain gang.

～

"TAKE THE WHEEL," RABBIT ORDERED TO GHOST. HE TOOK note of the wide smile that came with being in charge for just a few minutes while he walked the track.

"I'm on it!" He barked back and wondered what he could do with the few minutes in control. "You, you, post up on the track."

"White power!" The two selected exclaimed and rushed to carry out the duty. Not that one particularly needed security on the track. It was one of the more peaceful spots on the yard. Mainly because it was where the civilians and older guys converged. Many did their time walking in circles and plotting for success upon release.

Sa'id Salaam was often found there walking with his hands

behind his back with his lips moving even if alone. Most times he was reciting verses of the Qur'an to himself, other times it was the crazy characters in his head speaking. He did quite a bit of writing by first visualizing it in his head, then putting down on the paper.

Rabbit saw a familiar face looking at him each time it made a revolution around the circle. It took twenty minutes to trace the face back the twenty years. Then he stepped forward to speak. There was a slight stir when he began to approach but a wave of the hand settled it just as quickly.

"The infamous Rabbit," he greeted but didn't extend a hand for shaking.

"Fitz," Rabbit nodded and waited. There was a brief silence as both contemplated their next words and moves.

Fitz was a dangerous man in his own right, once upon a time. He was older now and would need help to bust a grape if that's what he wanted. He had plenty of help nearby since the Mexicans were all under him now.

Rabbit could easily whoop the man now and had his own crew not too far away. They all had eyes on him as they walked. Especially Ghost who assumed this meeting was business and not personal. His elation at being left in charge began to sour at being cut out of the meeting. He turned and saw One Eyed Dino nod as if he told him so.

"So, you don't deny it?" Fitz finally asked. He had dealt with many snitches in his sixty something years roaming the planet. Most will swear on everyone and everything they didn't tell.

"Not at all. I was a kid. You killed my dad," Rabbit admitted. Robert wasn't his biological father but still the only father he knew.

"It would have been honorable to kill me. I would have respected that," he sighed and shook his head.

"Again, I was a kid. Wasn't even jacking my dick yet," Rabbit repeated. He had ordered snitches killed during his time behind the wall and knew this could go bad.

" Agua bajo el puente," he said with another shrug before translating. "Water under the bridge. It is time to stop the killing. I have a chance to go home now. I would like to go home."

"Likewise," Rabbit said since he was up for parole now. Killing or being killed would ruin any chances he may have had at going home. Running the White Boys enabled him to amass a few hundred thousand dollars over the years. It could have been a few times that had he not been just and fair with his people.

Dino on the other hand had racked up just over a million because he was ruthless. The Bandos gave him the muscle he needed to operate in gang land. Likewise Rallo was shitting on his people and keeping the lions share of the proceeds. It was all he could manage to keep the connect paid.

The tense moment ended the moment the two bosses stopped and faced each other. Their eyes locked and their hands met. With that, twenty years of beef died and no one got killed.

Chapter Ten

"*C*layton. Detail!" The officer called through the intercom.

"Me?" Trouble asked Darius rhetorically and headed to the intercom to see what was going on. He pressed the button to summon the officer in the booth and repeated, "Me?"

"You're Clayton right? You're assigned to the chapel now," she explained and pressed the button to unlock the door.

"I gotta get straight. Give me a sec," he said and turned to do just that. One of the more notorious jackers managed to push the door and rushed out to the sweet spot so he could pull on his dick.

"Hope your damn dick come off in yo hand, you nasty bastard!" The woman shouted and he began to pull and twist on himself. She wouldn't write them up but didn't cooperate either. She blocked his view with folders but he didn't care. A dedicated jacker will jack off the essence left in the air from a woman passing by. Some would sniff a chair as soon as a woman stands from in and jack right there on the spot. Others jacked on the woman in the patrol car as it passed every few minutes. They jacked of commercials, sitcoms and especially the weather lady on the news. Yeah, its sick but not as sick as what was going on in some of the cells.

"What's up?" Darius asked when he rushed back in and

changed back into his uniform. Inmates were allowed to doff their state uniforms after four thirty. Most rocked shorts and t-shirts around the dorm to be comfortable.

"They put me in the chapel?" He asked but knew this had to be Stack's doing. He blessed him with the sweet detail after he departed.

"I have to work in the damn kitchen," Darius groaned.

"PBTP," Trouble laughed over his shoulder on his way out of the door. He saw the confused look on his face but he'd figure it out once he got there. The big girls were doing big business down in the kitchen. Jessie was strictly giving head since the pussy belonged to Trouble.

"Yo, I'm coming out!" Trouble announced before stepping out into the hallway. He was giving the jacker notice to put his dick away. If he didn't they would fight right there on the spot. Then the jacker would get jumped and stabbed by the Riders and never allowed back on compound.

"Sup bruh," the jacker greeted with his dick away and hands up to show respect. Respect is a big deal behind the wall. Aretha made a hit song out of those letters, but they will get you sent 'out back' in here. Trouble nodded and kept it moving. The man waited until he was completely out of sight before picking up where he left off.

"Nasty bastard!" The officer grimaced when he resumed.

"What up yo! The brother Stack told me you was coming," New York greeted and extended his hand.

"Sup," Trouble greeted back and shook it like Darius had been teaching him. He was eager to join this new world of eye contact and handshakes. Bank accounts and business deals as opposed to shoot outs and drug deals.

"Chap wanna holla at you before we get started," New York said and nodded towards her door. He resumed setting up the chairs for service. Social distancing meant setting them far enough to prevent guys from giving each other hand jobs while Chaplain gave her soul music rendition of the gospel.

"Knock, knock," Trouble announced from the open door way.

"Come on in Mr. Clayton," Chaplain Gayle greeted and stood to get a good look at him. "Close that door behind you."

"Yes ma'am," he said and compiled.

"Let me see yo hand?" She asked and he produced them. Inmates who smoke have yellow, brown or black finger tips depending on how much they smoke. He assumed that's what she was checking for until she squirted some oil into his palm.

"Huh?" Trouble asked since this was his first time coming to church.

"Go on. Get yaself straight!" She urged. Trouble wouldn't have known what she meant if she hadn't been staring down at his crotch.

"Oh, no ma'am. I'm good!" He swore. He left off the part of the pounds of pussy Jessie gave him earlier.

"Oh, OK then. It's good for your waves too. So it don't go to waste," she advised.

"Thanks," Trouble said as he rubbed the oil into his palms and smoothed it over his waves.

"Help him set up. Once we get started you keep an eye on the bathroom. One man at a time. They'll fuck you know!" She informed wide eyed and made him laugh.

"Yes ma'am!" He chuckled and got to work. New York showed him the ropes and they made it through their first night. A few guys wanted to try the bathroom but Trouble's presence was a deterrent. They couldn't punk the shot caller so they would have to figure something else out.

"Good job gentleman," Chaplain Gayle gushed after her Motown medley.

"Thank you ma'am," they both sang in chorus. She looked both ways before passing them both a chicken sandwich. They hit their chorus once more, "Thank you!"

"Here you go son," New York said and passed his sandwich off to Trouble.

"What's wrong with them?" Trouble reeled. Free world food was too hard to get to be turning down.

"Nothing. My people be bringing me food!" He explained which is explained why he was in a rush to get back to the dorm. He and Lalonda hadn't crossed any lines but he enjoyed her mama's biscuits.

~

"Sssss, mmmm, Mmhm. You like that? You like this dick?" An inmate asked as he pulled and twisted on his erection.

It was bright and shiny courtesy of a squirt of baby oil from the bottle he kept in his pocket. Most real 'jackers' keep a bottle on them at all times since they'll jack anywhere, and any time. Others kept a glob of grease behind an ear for that same purpose. Or a glob behind each ear if they're really about that jack life.

Lalonda stopped writing disciplinary reports after catching a man choking on another man. Still she usually ignored the men who slivered into the sweet spot to jack off while peeking at her in the booth. Today she decided to take a peep herself. The peep turned into a look, then she just watched. Word got out and dudes waited in line to show her what they had.

"Right here," Lalonda dared through the glass and stuck her tongue out. She was lucky she was behind that glass to because the flirt caused the man to explode instantly. His knees buckled and he skeeted high enough to reach the glass.

"Fuck!" He exclaimed and slid down the wall. He would have fell asleep right there if not for the line behind him.

"Nuh-uh shawty! My next!" A young Roller demanded. As bad as he wanted a nap right then, right there, he didn't want to get stabbed so he moved on.

"Let me ride with you?" His partner asked.

"Come on!" He agreed. It wasn't uncommon for the young ones to jack together off a woman or even on a phone while watching porn. They didn't even realize how gay that was. Or, maybe they did. The two boys gathered round the booth and pulled on their peckers like if they were racing. They giggled and stroked while Lalonda did her paperwork. She gave an occasional glance that made them giggle and skeet.

"Next," she laughed to herself. She laughed again when a seventy year old came out. Paw Paw wanted to get his rocks off too, so she let him. Lalonda was really passing time until evening church call was over. That's when her buddy would return from his detail. She would lock the doors and spend her shift kicking it with him.

"Officer Stanton," New York greeted after returning to the dorm. He made sure to put a little extra 'up top' in it since she loved his accent so much.

"Hey New York" She giggled like a girl with a crush. Mainly because she was a girl with a crush. Her husband made her feel smaller than a baby ant by cheating on her with the big girl. New York looked her in her eyes when he spoke, smiled and always complimented her. All she needed to feel like a woman again.

"You smell good," he gushed since he knew compliment go a long way. She giggled and cooed just like he knew she would.

"Me or my mama biscuits?" She dared and twisted her lips. She made sure to bring him some every day after Shay told her how much they made her day when she was down. She did the baking sometimes but it was still mama's recipe. He could tell the difference but never said a word.

"Definitely you! You smell edible too," he laughed. She didn't though and looked dead serious at the statement. "My bad! I ain't mean, like, not, I'm saying."

"I get it," she said and twisted her lips. Malcolm was one of them country boys who didn't eat pussy much. Birthdays and anniversaries but then again she didn't go down on him much either. She had seen more blow jobs during rounds around here than in her household.

"Well, I better, yeah," he said and picked his broom up to sweep the hall and mop the 'sweet spot'.

"Yeah they went crazy today!" She said, but left out how turned on she got seeing all those different dicks. She had seen short dicks that barely extended past the fist to long dicks that took two hands to stroke. There were thick dicks, thin dicks and dicks with curves. Some bent upward, others bent down.

One had a curve and a bend like something a woman could buy in a sex shop. Some skeeted high as the glass, while others came with a slow dribble. She had seen it all today.

"I bet. A beautiful, fine woman working!" He said as he grabbed the supplies from the closet. This compliment put a wicked grin on her face.

"Come here," she ordered before he could step out of the mop closet. He followed directions and she shoved her tongue inside of his mouth.

"Mmmmm," New York moaned and massaged her round ass as their tongues swirled in each others mouths. Lalonda suddenly pulled away and looked at him. New York was ready to apologize and run but she had made her decision.

"Hurry up," she whispered wickedly as she unbuckled her uniform pants. It wasn't until she pulled them down and turned around that he realized this was happening.

"Ok then!" He cheered happily and whipped out the dick. It had been the whole five years he'd been gone since he saw some pussy so he bent down to take a look. It had been them same five years since he tasted some pussy so he leaned in and took a lick.

"Ssssss!" Lalonda hissed when his tongue touched her lonely vagina. It was so clean and fresh he couldn't pull away even if he wanted to. He didn't want to so he continued to suck on it like a mango until she came in his mouth. "Fuck me!"

"Oh, I'm about to fuck you!" He shot back and took position behind her. Her vagina was super slick and slippery from her juices and his saliva so he slid right in. "About to fuck you real good!"

"Mmm!" She moaned as he filled her up. He wasn't quite as large as her husband but she was good and tight from lack of action. "Get, this, pu.... Huh?"

"Arghh! Ugh! Mmmm, shit!" New York moaned and groaned as he filled her box with little New Yorkers. After the mighty declaration of fucking her real good, he only managed to fuck her real quick. That good pussy will do that though but New York held on.

Lalonda felt he stayed hard so she gently massaged his dick with her vaginal muscles. He slowly pulled out, then pushed back in. Out, in, out, in, wiggle, out and back in. Soon he had a full fledged stroke going on. She showed her appreciation by coating his dick in that good creamy goodness good pussy produces.

"Awe man, I'm finna come," Lalonda moaned as if it were a problem. It may have been because as soon as she did her already tight box contracted and convulsed, causing him to bust another nut inside the woman.

"Shit baby!" New York groaned as he let loose the juice. He stayed put until he was drained and began to deflate.

"I needed that," Lalonda admitted more to herself than him.

"Shit, you?" He laughed. Five years is a long time to go without sex. Dudes need to consider that along with the pros and cons of that next lick. Five, ten, twenty years to life with no pussy is a hell of a crime deterrent.

"We probably shouldn't do this anymore?" She asked.

"Probably not," he agreed as they cleaned themselves up. It sounded pretty convincing except they did it two more times that night.

Chapter Eleven

"*Y*ou guys ready?" The jail officer asked as he arrived at the cell holding the two killers. They seemed like anything but killers reading together from a text book.

Connor took Fuck-Shit's illiteracy personal and personally set out to fix it. Likewise, Fuck-Shit proved it was his circumstances that corrupted him, not his color. He wanted to read and everything else life had to offer. They just didn't offer it in his hood very much. A crack addict mother, absentee father and neglect set him on the path of fuck shit.

"Yeah, I mean, yes," Fuck-Shit replied and stood. He was facing the rest of his life behind bars but was remarkably calm about it.

"We are," Connor sighed and stood as well. His fate was somewhat worse since the district attorney decided to seek the death penalty. Not that the case warranted it, he just didn't get much action down here and never had a chance to seek it before.

Connor too had accepted his fate. Dying with his rectum fully intact was worth every volt of electricity the electric chair had to offer. He killed for what was his and had no problem dying about it. The men were cuffed and shackled for the long trip across the street. It was only across the street but that's equivalent to several miles when your ankles are shackled a few inches apart.

"OK guys. Your lawyers will be in to see you," the court deputy explained as he put them in separate rooms. He removed the shackles from their ankles and seated them inside.

'They tried me up!' Fuck-Shit thought to himself as he looked at the open ground floor window. His wrist were still cuffed but he could run like that. Life on the run beat life behind the wall so he stood and looked around.

'Inna mal usri yusra' popped in his head when he lifted his foot to walk to the window. He remembered the last sermon Sa'id gave about this verse of the Qur'an. It translated to, 'with difficulty comes ease' and eased back in his chair.

"Awe man, he sat back down," the sniper moaned from his perch across the street. They didn't get much excitement around here and gunning an escaping murderer down would have given them some action.

"May as well send his lawyer in then," the deputy sighed. Fuck-Shit may have had better luck out the window with the sniper than in court with the public defender. The disheveled man was another part of the plan since he didn't have a clue about the case until a few minutes ago.

"OK, let me try this," the skinny man with wrinkled clothes announced and bared his stained teeth in his attempt to sound out his five syllable name. "La-la-don't-ah, don, don q, qua..."

"Ladonquavious," Fuck-Shit sighed and looked over at the window again.

"Yeah that! You people have the most difficult names! Was there some sort of contest for longest name or..." The man asked oblivious to the frustration on his client's face. "Well, anyway. We'll plead guilty and just throw ourselves on the mercy of the court."

"You don't even wanna know what happened?" Fuck-Shit asked. Not that he would tell him but he at least wanted to be heard out.

"Well, they have the video," he explained and fumbled to

get his phone out. He turned the video on but it was still tuned to trailer trash gone wild. A dirty butt blonde was busy bobbing her head of a car. The lawyer got stuck and forgot what he was doing.

"Say shawty?" Fuck-Shit called to summon him back to the matter at hand.

"Oh, yes. The uh, video..." He said and pulled up the clip. It was cued up to the point where Fuck-Shit walked up to George and stabbed him.

"So, the mercy of the court?" He asked since the video looked so bad.

Connor on the other hand was fairing a lot better with his high priced lawyer. The man had already gotten him a sweetheart deal on one body and planned on eating the case for lunch. The district attorney had five corpses and some gory pics but Connor's lawyer had done his homework.

"This is supposed to be a preliminary hearing but we motion to drop all charges!" Mr. McDougall said and adjusted his glasses.

"Drop, charges?" The judge asked in return. He had to split the words up to even get them out of his mouth. This was the most excitement they had around here in forever. The prison had been simply sweeping bodies under the rug and burying them out back. "Are you telling me, that these five men don't deserve justice?"

"That's exactly what I'm telling you! Nathaniel Bartholomew the third, also known as Nasty Nate. He was convicted in nineteen eighty five for two counts of murder. Served twenty years and released on parole. He killed three people this time and received three life sentences without parole. Since he's been incarcerated he's amassed a record of fifty two rapes and three more homicides. He belongs to a gang named, the Booty Bandits. No one we've interviewed ha anything nice to say about him at all. Except for one man who said, and I quote, 'Nasty Nate shole can eat ass'."

"Well they don't call him nasty for nothing," the judge agreed.

"No sir, they don't. Next was Tommy Mack. Four counts

of aggravated child molestation. Rape, kidnapping..." Mr. McDougall said. He laid out the dastardly records of all of the dead men and bust a B-boy stance at the prosecutor like, 'how you like me now'.

"Well, just because they were bad people didn't mean uh, they deserve to um, sheesh, uh, die," the prosecutor sighed. He had trouble getting that bullshit out of his mouth since he didn't believe it much himself. They all needed dead and got it.

"Uh yes it does," McDougall chimed back in. "The five rushed into my clients cell and attacked him with knives. Given their records, if safe to say we know what they came for. They couldn't have it, my client protected his, uh, property to the utmost of his ability!"

"As he should. Case is dismissed!" The judge said and banged his gavel. All was not lost since they still had Fuck-Shit and his wack ass public defender.

"You done?" Fuck-Shit asked as they passed each other in the isle.

"Done!" Connor cheered. He had missed out on going to the halfway house but still only had a few weeks left to serve. They would be spent in protective custody since the rest of the Bandos would certainly murder him on sight.

"That's good man," the kid said and hung his head as he followed his dirty, wrinkled lawyer to the front of the courtroom.

"What was that?" Mr. McDougall asked as they left the courtroom. He knew Fuck-Shit was the defendant but why was he with the janitor was what he wanted to know.

"Maaaannnn," Connor drawled and spelled it all out.

"State of Georgia vs la-donna' la quash..." The court clerk attempted.

"You'll never get it!" The lawyer laughed. "He pleads guil..."

"One second your honor!" Mr. McDougall announced as he stormed back into courtroom. He marched up to the table and mushed the lawyer out the way like KRS-ONE did PM Dawn off the stage once upon a time. "I'll be representing..."

"Ladonquavious Smith!" Fuck-Shit adlibbed like a rapper's hype man. They bumped fists and he went on.

"My client pleads not guilty!" He declared. He knew none of the details but knew he could do better than a blind plea.

"Perhaps this fancy smancy city lawyer would like to look at the video?" The country bumpkin of a prosecutor bragged and hit play. All heads turned to the large screen on the wall. Everyone saw the defendant stab the man, who fell dead.

"Cool but, can I see the whole tape?" McDougall asked.

"Huh?" The prosecution asked as if he didn't hear. The lawyer repeated his request and the judge gave the order. "Side bar your honor?"

"Come," the judge ordered and the lawyers began to approach. "Just the state!"

"That's highly inappropriate!" McDougall dared.

"Yeah well..." The judge shrugged since he didn't care much about procedure. The lawyer strained his ears to ear the whispers of the judge and prosecutor as he planned to file complaints. That wouldn't be necessary once the prosecutor spoke again for the record.

"Move to dismiss the charges," he said. The words were barely out of his mouth before the judge chimed in.

"Granted. Case dismissed!" he said and banged his gavel. Both Fuck-Shit and McDougall looked at each other in shock. The lawyer planned to argue for a manslaughter charge that would cost the kid twenty years of his life. A high price indeed but cheaper than a life sentence.

"What does that mean?" Fuck-shit asked, seeking clarity.

"That means you've been spared. Don't waste the blessing!" he said and shook his hand.

"I won't. In sha Allah, I won't!" he vowed and meant every word.

⁓

"As salaamu alaykum brother Sa'id!" Sa'id heard behind him as he walked the track. He ignored the frustration of being pulled back into prison in favor of returning the greeting since it's actually mandatory. So much so he began returning it before turning to see who he was speaking too.

"Wa alaykum as salaam! Oh shit! What's up lil bruh!" He cheered when he saw Fuck-Shit. "How did you make out?"

"That shit was crazy akhi!" Fuck-Shit recalled and grimaced as he tried to make sense of it once again. He couldn't so he passed it over to the sheikh to see if he could explain it. "One minute I had some dusty, wrinkled public pretender. Finna cop out to the charge and get a life damn sentence..."

"And then?" Sa'id asked since the memory had taken him back into the courtroom.

"Oh, my bad. Then next thing I know, some high price lawyer mush dude out the way. He said something, they said something, then the judge was like, 'case dismissed'," he explained. He did take it to the right person since Sa'id knew exactly what happened.

"Allah said whoever believes in Him, keeps his duty to Him, and puts his trust in Him, He will help them out of every difficulty and provide from sources they never could imagine," he relayed.

"Facts! Cuz I was making my five salats err day! And Connor taught me how to read better so I was reading my Qur'an!" The youth added happily. Then a look of concern spread on his graffiti riddled face. "Ain't you worried someone finna complain 'bout you always talking 'bout Islam in yo books tho?"

"Nope. Fuck them folks! I'm a Muslim, that's gonna be seen in everything I do!" Sa'id said and meant. Islam is every second, every breath and only the devil has problems with the mention of God. "Anyway, where they put you?"

"Man, I'm in the dorm with the so-called Imam," he said like he just bit into something bitter. Sa'id let out a sigh and wondered if he should even ask. He didn't have to since the young brother went on. "They don't even pray akh!"

"Chill lil bruh. We don't wanna get into back biting," he warned since the sin is on the one who listens as much as the one who does it.

"But akh, he be having punks in and out of his room! I went to get him for salat and his room smell like smoke!" Fuck-Shit lamented.

"Have patience akhi," Sa'id reminded since patience is highly recommended in every religion. Even he had to wonder if the time of patience had morphed into the time for action. Prison is a fishbowl and no one can do anything without someone seeing them. If someone sees something they will definitely say something. He had heard the whispers in the wind but didn't act without proof.

"In sha Allah," the kid said and smiled. The light of faith made his smile just a little brighter.

Chapter Twelve

"*You* look, different. Happy even," Shay asked and squinted to see if she could place the emotion on her sister in law's face.

"I am!" Lalonda admitted and stifled a laugh. She was completely giddy and that can only come from one place.

"Oooh! Oooh!" Shay exclaimed and pointed. "You gave that man some coochie didn't you! Yeah you did! Un-huh! You been doing the nasty at work!"

"Shush girl! You finna tell the whole world!" She shushed since the outburst turned a few heads in the restaurant. Shay mean mugged the nosey patrons back into their own business so they could continue.

"Girl!" She gushed both happy and scared. She knew the woman was lonely but didn't want her to get into trouble either.

"I'm sorry, but I needed that!" Lalonda said with 'not sorry' on her face. "Shoot, he ate me like one of mama biscuits!"

"Damn! That's some good eating!" Shay shot back and cracked them up. "So, where y'all did it? How y'all did it? Don't leave nothing out!"

"Well..." She began and ended with the last mutual climax before her shift ended. They did it again the next shift as well as the one after that. She was off for a few days but had every intention of doing it again once she got back to work.

"Dang!" Shay sang wide eyed with excitement. She wished she crossed that line with Chuck but losing her virginity on her wedding night was better. "So, what about Malcolm?"

"What about him? This is his doing!" She shot back correctly because had he been treating her correctly she wouldn't be in this position. Nor any of the positions they managed in the mop closet.

"He still ain't signed the papers?" Shay asked to see if anything had changed since last week's luncheon.

"No! I seen that square booty Sheryl in the Piggly Wiggly and started to tell her to tell her man to give me my divorce! Shoot, my man getting out next month. I'm trying to be with him!" She revealed to them both at the same time. Lalonda's vagina was directly connected to her heart. They were a package deal. As it should be.

"Wow!" Shay reeled and muted herself before saying more than she should.

"Wow is right, so y'all can stop paying my bills," Lalonda said and cocked her head, daring her to deny it. The last time she went to pay her lights, cable and phone she found zero balances. The same thing happened with the gas bill and car note.

"Well, hmp, OK," was Shay's reply. She stuffed some of S&S's world famous chicken into her mouth to prevent anything from coming out. Prison taught her a lot of things. Minding her own business was among the top of the lessons learned.

"Anyway, can I ask you a personal question?" Lalonda asked but didn't wait for an answer. "You be sucking my brother's thang?"

"Like a damn blow pop! Like that thang is oxygen and I'm finna die! Like..." Shay laughed until getting tuned out. Lalonda had heard enough and New York had a blow job in his near future. As soon as she got home she hit the porn sites for pointers.

∽

"CLAYTON, VISIT," THE OFFICER CALLED. IT ACTUALLY CAME AS a shock since Malaysia had this, that and the other thing that prevented her from coming down for the last few weeks. The money was good so he was good. Jessie kept him good in her snug, warm, big girl box so he had no complaints.

"Mind if I use the phone?" Darius asked needlessly since Trouble always left it with him.

"Yeah," he said and passed it. Malaysia said she wasn't coming but no one else ever came so he got fresh to see his woman. "Mph!"

"What?" Darius asked of the huff. Trouble shook his head and continued to prepare. A few minutes later he headed to the door and got buzzed out.

Troubled traipsed over to the visitation area reminding himself not to be petty. She was more comfortable lying about not moving on with her life than being honest about it. It saw all the signs as well as her excuses not to come the last few weeks.

What he couldn't see was her plots to keep him there longer rather than home sooner. She hoped he would kill Rallo when she told him but he didn't. Again when they put Bama at the camp and still he did nothing. Did nothing so he could get home to her while she was scheming against him.

Malaysia wasn't showing yet, but being pregnant didn't sit well with her, sitting across from him for hours. He would remember her quirks of pregnancy and figure it out. That would be the only way he would find out because she had no intention on telling him. There was only a third of the money put up since she spent it almost as fast as it was coming in. He even started sifting some aside to let big Jessie hold since Malaysia was harder to contact sometimes. Ironically Malaysia was actually in town since she rode down with Pablo to bring the work to Jessie. Seeing the big girl he was paying for sex made her even angrier. That took more shopping trips to make her feel better.

"Huh?" Trouble asked as he scanned the visitors rooms

and didn't see who he was looking for. He actually looked over his granny twice before he registered. It then registered who his visitors were. "Oooh!"

"Boy let me find out you done forgot yo ole granny!" The woman fussed and scooped him into a hug.

"Never that! I just thought, never mind," he said and hugged her back.

"Mmhm!" Reecie hummed like she had a secret. She did and it was eating her alive to keep it. She hadn't actually kept since she shared the video with a few people.

"Hey lil cuz. See you knocked up again," he cheered and hugged her too.

"Mmhm, hmp!" She hummed and huffed.

"Boy them dogs was just barking at me when we came in!" Granny fussed.

"Cuz you smell like weed granny," he laughed and sniffed across the empty table.

"Anyway boy! What you want to eat?" She laughed and stood. Granny had rode a few bids with a few dudes over the decades so she knew the routine. She brought plenty of quarters in a plastic bag to feed her baby.

"Them jalapeño burgers!" He gushed. He ate plenty of free world food between Jessie and various officers but those jalapeño burgers were the shit.

"Ooh get something for the baby too!" Reecie pleaded. She always asked for the baby but she was the one who ate it.

"Speaking of babies, why y'all ain't go scoop up lil Trevor?" He asked since he missed his son. Malaysia didn't need to come as long as he could see his son. Many a man has built bonds with their kids from across the small table.

"Mph! Mmhm! Hmp!" She huffed and twisted in her seat.

"Just tell me," he sighed since he knew her well enough to know what all the huffing and puffing was about.

"Malaysia got a boyfriend! I seent them screwing in the car!" She blurted as it were painful to hold in any longer.

"Yeah, I knew that. Ion care," he shrugged. "Why the car tho?"

"Cuz he was dropping some money off. She went out and

rode his dick in the front seat like....uh'uh, uh," she said and demonstrated how to ride a dick in the front seat.

"Money?" Trouble wondered. Different scenarios ran through his mind as to why whoever he was would be dropping money off. His head nodded when he remembered how good, and tight, and hot the pussy was. That'll get some money dropped off for sure.

"What's wrong with you boy?" Granny asked when she returned with the food. She raised him so she knew how he looked when he wanted to cry.

"Huh? Nothing..." He said and bit into the steaming, hot burger to change the subject.

"I gotta pee!" Reecie announced and danced in her seat once again.

"Over there," he pointed. Reecie jumped up and rushed to relieve her bladder.

"Look,'" granny began once they were alone. She had done this enough to know what she was seeing from the sidelines. "Lay-lay is a baby. A baby cain't do no bid. They can hardly keep they drawers on when they man in town."

"I ain't stutting no dang Malaysia!" He huffed sounding just like he did many moons ago when they were kids. Granny was right though so he manned up and moved on. Darius was opening a whole new world to him and he was eager to enter it.

∾

"WAIT, HOLE UP!" LIL-ZAY SCRAMBLED TO PAUSE THE VIDEO when Trouble walked into his cell.

"Let me find out y'all looking at chicks with dicks!" he laughed half joking since oddly enough some men did. One of life's many contradictions that it just wasn't meant for him to understand.

"Naw shawty it's..." Lo began but got cut off before he could explain. He had seen enough shit he didn't need to see borrowing phones and wanted to clear his name.

"Shut the fuck up my nigga!" Zay fussed like he wander to fight.

"Show me," Trouble demanded softly. He was one of those leaders who commanded respect without having to raise his voice or make threats. He still managed to have violators fucked up without it. Lil-Zay let out a big sigh as he turned the phone to Trouble and hit play.

Trouble felt a large hand take hold on his heart when he saw Malaysia riding a dick in a front seat. It didn't come as a complete surprise since Reecie told him about it. That also explained who recorded it but seeing it threatened to kill him dead on the spot. Every dude claims they don't care what they chick do until they actually see it. Now he was seeing the only woman he loved in ecstasy as she rocked on the next man's dick. He couldn't hear her but knew the 'sssss' and 'shit!' that was coming out of her mouth. He also knew the look on her face when she was about to come. The same look on her face right now.

"I bet that pussy good!" Lo blurted and covered his mouth with his own hand when he remembered who she was.

"Shit it is!" Trouble said like the capital G he was. "Shit about this tight!"

"Damn!" Lil-Zay exclaimed as his boss held his fingers in a circle he couldn't see through. He had fucked a few chicks in his life but none that tight.

"Where y'all get that from anyway?" Trouble asked offhandedly, like he didn't care. He leaned in and squinted at the back of the man's head but couldn't make him out. He knew the make of the car but Pablo bought this Benz after he had gotten locked up.

"That shit on the net," Lo shrugged. A popular porn site specialized in homemade clips like this. Trouble took note and headed down to his cell.

"Hey, I gotta go," Darius announced to the person on the other end of the line when Trouble walked in. Trouble waved him off so he didn't rush but he had already hung up. "I appreciate it."

"My pleasure," Trouble replied. It didn't necessarily fit this instance but he liked how it sounded when Darius said it. He noticed the man always said 'please', 'thank you' and 'my pleasure' in his every day conversation.

"Had a good visit?" He asked since it wasn't clear from the look on his face. Darius had plenty of people to talk to on the phone but none came for a visit.

"Huh?" He asked meaning no since Reecie broke the news to him. It definitely softened the blow of what he saw so he changed his mind. "It was great. My grandmother and cousin."

"Cool," Darius nodded and stood to leave. He knew Trouble would want to change out of his crispy white visitation uniform into some shorts. He did but hit the porn site first. Malaysia's clip was listed by her name which meant it was personal. He searched a few more names he knew and got a few more hits.

"Damn lil girl!" He reeled at Reecie's small collection of videos. Most were hotels or the VIP room at the Chili Pepper. It wasn't a good look for the girl but could possibly help identify whoever left the baby in her belly.

"Hmp?" Trouble guessed because Trouble was a smart man. He finished changing and set off in search of his hunch. He grabbed a joint to smoke and a sack of meth for bait before heading out.

"Dis nigga," Gip groaned when Trouble popped up at his cell.

"Dis the nigga that made you look different," Trouble laughed in his face and waited to see if he wanted to miss another store call because he couldn't log onto the kiosk. He was already in a foul mood after watching Malaysia coming all over the next man's dick. Gip didn't want that smoke so he tucked his tail and departed.

"Gotta watch him cuz. He treacherous," Rallo laughed. He was half playing but the kid was dangerous.

"Yeah I know. He fucked my knuckles up bad last time," he replied and passed the joint.

"I heard you went to visit?" Rallo asked as he lit the weed. He of course heard since they were in the same dorm and the officer called it out through the intercom. Rallo had never had visit himself even though they shared the same grandmother who made the two hour drive to see him. Proof that people will look out for you the same way you looked out for them. Trouble helped her out on the streets and behind the wall. She would have driven two days to check on her baby.

"Yeah, granny 'ndem," he replied but he already knew that since Reecie can't hold water.

"Malaysia ain't come again?" Rallo asked and passed the smoldering weed. Trouble squinted to see if he was being sarcastic because she came in the video or if he meant came for a visit. Sarcasm is actually a sign of intelligence so he obviously meant the visit.

"Naw, she be busy," he said and regretted it instantly.

"Like a mug! I saw the video," Rallo laughed. He had been waiting for his opening to put it out there and there it was.

"Yeah, I saw that," Trouble shrugged like a G. "It's her pussy, she can do what she want with it."

"Facts cuz! I may have to hit that myself when I touch the turf," he said and watched for a reaction. Trouble was smarter than him though and didn't give him. He was also smart enough to pursue his GED and work his details. Everything he needed to do for early release. Especially not laying a hand on the snitch Bama.

"Yard call!" The officer announced, setting off a chorus of men repeating it. Trouble dropped the sack of dope when he stood and watched Rallo's eyes follow it. He didn't alert his family that he dropped it, but that's why he did it. Just a little help towards his self destruction.

Chapter Thirteen

"*Man* this ain't right!" Fuck-Shit groaned as he stood ready for prayer. He was in the dorm with several other Muslims yet none of them showed up. Not to mention the prayer leader but he never came out of his cell to lead the prayer.

Fuck-Shit knew Jahil sold drugs and had the other brothers in the dorm working for him. Some sold, others provided protection since the Rollers were getting bolder by the second. Their recklessness increased with their numbers. If they ever became the dominant gang the chain gang was in trouble.

He saw a sissy called Pudding go into Jahil's room and put the flap up. He tried to make excuses for his brother but also knew the best way to avoid suspicion was not to be yourself in suspicious situations. Behind a closed door with a sissy and the flap up was suspect as fuck. Still, he wasn't concerned with all that. All Fuck-Shit wanted was the extra blessing that came from praying in congregation verses praying alone.

With that in mind he headed up to the Imam's cell to remind him of the prayer. Allah revealed that reminding benefits the believers so he approached the door. He saw the flap wasn't all the way up which left a gap. There was a moment of pause while he recalled that spying was forbidden.

"So is the shit they be doing," he reasoned and took a peep. Somethings shouldn't be seen since they can't be unseen. What was going on in that cell was one of them. He heard himself screech as he fell away. "Aaaaah!"

"What's up akh!" One of the other bothers demanded and rushed to his side. All Fuck-Shit could do was point at the door.

"Fuck you got going on!" Jahil snapped as he rushed out. His erection was still erect after quickly tucking it into his pants. The scream caused him to look up and see the one eye seeing him through the gap in the flap while he was doing what he was doing.

"You, I, he..." Fuck-Shit stammered trying to vocalize what he saw. That's exactly what Jahil didn't want to happen.

"Y'all beat this nigga and put him on the door!" He ordered. The other brothers liked the kid but liked the dirty money even more.

"Sorry akh," one said and swung on him. Fuck-Shit fought as best he could but there were too many. Jahil made it one less as he went back into his cell and finished what he had started.

"A'ight, I'ma go!" Fuck-Shit conceded and balled up halfway through the halfhearted beat down. The brothers knew what Jahil was into but none of them feared Allah as He should be feared. The Prophet Muhammad peace be upon him once said, 'if you have no shame, do as you want'. These were them dudes.

"Just business," another brother offered apologetically and helped him to his feet. Everyone is a slave to something and his master was money. Still he helped the kid pack his belongings and move to the next dorm.

～

"As salaamu alaykum. What happened to you?" Shakur greeted and asked when the lumped up brother arrived at his dorm. He may have been old but didn't play when it came to his brothers.

"Nothing," The brother helping with his stuff said and dipped his head in shame and turned to leave. Shakur twisted his lips dubiously at the youngster to decide if he could stay in there with him.

"Don't come in here with the, fuck shit," the elder fussed.

"I wasn't! Wallahi, dem brothers ain't right!" He moaned and actually shed a tear on the spot. Tears and sincerity go hand in hand so he grabbed his stuff and helped him to his new cell.

"They got you in here with one of dem, white boys," Shakur growled. He was one of those older Muslims who came up through the different phases of Islam in America. Starting with the nation until the founder's own son declared that to be some bullshit. He followed him in that which was better for a few years before being guided to that which was best. The best of speech is the book of Allah and the best of guidance in the example of His final Messenger, Muhammad, peace be upon him. He now practiced Orthodox Islam in its purest form.

"He ain't gay is he!" Fuck-Shit stopped in his tracks and demanded.

"What happened over there?" Shakur demanded. They put his stuff into his new cell and the kid filled him in. The shit had officially hit the fan, now someone had to clean it up.

∾

"Awe hell," Sa'id sighed when he spotted Shakur marching towards him with the youngster in tow. That would usually mean Fuck-Shit had done some fuck shit but the kid had been on his best behavior lately.

"As salaamu alaykum! Tell him, what you told me!" Shakur demanded hotly. "Go on, tell him!"

"What happened?" He asked as he surveyed the knots on the kids head.

"Man, I was tryna offer salah, and no one would come, so I went to get them, and I went to the Imam room, and the flap was up, but it wasn't all the up, and, so I looked under it, and I saw Pudding on his knees and..."

"Hole up akhi. This is a very serious matter. Perhaps you didn't see exactly what you thought you saw?" Sa'id offered. It was a very serious matter indeed and he would have to act on it.

"It was from under the flap," Shakur added as well.

"Bruh, he had his dick in the punk mouth! Ain't no confusing that for something else. You cain't accidentally put yo dick in someone mouth!" Fuck-Shit fumed. He was hot about what he saw but even hotter if they were going to sweep it under the rug.

He may have been new to the faith but was pretty sure you can't be a gay Imam. He was right, you can't. Nor should the Imam be engaged in selling or using drugs of any kind. While people are human an humans have problems, those people should step aside and not lead the prayer. No one is perfect but Jahil wasn't even trying to do better. He used his position to pad his pockets. A bunch of insincere brothers acted as his security in exchange for drugs and money.

"Nah, can't accidentally do that," Sa'id and Shakur agreed in unison. They looked at each other and shook their heads.

"It's time to step up akhi," the elder advised.

"It's time to go home," Sa'id countered. It was but first he had to fix this. The religion had been hijacked and he wouldn't leave the sincere brothers in that state.

Chapter Fourteen

---

*Y*ard call was announced and most of the prison population set out in search of some sunlight. Some wanted to work out while others played ball. The gangs always went out too in hopes something would pop off. A bunch of young men with little to do is a recipe for disaster.

"Bruh, I know dat nigga from some where...'" Bama said as he watched Darius complete a lap on the track. He usually spent his yard call minding his business while running the track.

"Shit that's cuz bunk mate," Rallo said with a smile. He knew Bama had a vendetta against the Riders in general and Trouble in particular.

Trouble did all he could to prevent Lil-Zay from killing the snitch for fear of it falling back on him. A war would come back on him but everyone respected a one on one. This was prison, men are going to fight. As long as no one got jumped on or stabbed the administration didn't care. Bama took advantage of the situation by calling out Riders any chance he got. He had beat a couple up already but had his sights set on Trouble. He clearly wanted some trouble.

"Yeah, I know this nigga. He the police!" Bama announced the next time Darius made a pass. He was a civilian so he could be jumped on without starting a war. The

SA'ID SALAAM

Rollers all rolled down from their bleacher to wait on him to
come around again.

"The Rollers moving..." One of the Riders alerted when
the gang made their move.

"Shit we need to ride on all them fuck niggas!" Zay fumed.
He didn't like any of them but particularly Bama for snitching
and beating up a few of his brothers.

"Not yet. Just chill," Trouble advised but kept his eye on
the Rollers. He missed the daggers being shot at his back from
Lil-Zay.

"Bruh, mash the button so we can smash these niggas!" He
pleaded. The meth running through his system had him antsy
and ready to do something.

"They pressing up on my bunk-mate!" Trouble said when
they surrounded Darius when he made it back around.

"He ain't no Rider big bruh!" Zay snapped. Two Riders
had black eyes but he was ready to protect a civilian. What
they couldn't understand was how much Trouble was learning
from the man. He introduced him to a whole new world and
he would protect his interest.

"Y'all stay here then!" Trouble snapped back and headed
over. His loyal soldiers stayed put but only because that was
the order he gave. They still kept their eyes on him without
blinking. If anything popped off they would coming running.

"What's up fellas?" Darius asked when he was surrounded
by Rollers. He was too green to recognize the danger he was
in. When the knives and ice picks appeared he got the picture.
His bladder suddenly felt full and threatened to pee down
his leg.

"My Roller say you the police!" Rallo barked and nodded
towards Bama.

"Yeah you is!" He said and moved to pop it off. "I know yo
ass!"

"Y'all hole up!" Trouble barked as he slid in between
them. "What y'all fucking with bruh 'fo?"

"He a cop!" Bama repeated and stepped closer like he
wanted trouble with Trouble too. The whole yard turned their
attention to the track to see how this would play out.

92

"Good job niggers," Rabbit laughed. As long as the blacks stayed divided his White Boys had the power. It always baffled him how ferocious they fought each other. He wondered if niggers hate each other as much as racist whites do. They do, even more so. Just listen to the latest hit song at the moment, any moment.

"Wait..." Trouble said and paused to laugh in his face. "I knooooooow you not calling nobody no police!"

"Oooh," Rallo instigated. Bama was ignorant enough to take the bait.

"Shoot a one then! If not, we finna kill this nigga!" Bama dared. Trouble knew Bama and knew he was a killer.

"Shit I'll shoot a one with you, but y'all gonna leave my bunk-mate alone! He ain't in the streets. I talk to the man's family, he ain't no police!" Trouble said in Darius's defense. He hadn't actually spoken to his family but heard him on the phone with them daily.

"Fuck this!" Gutta said and stepped down from the Riders bleachers. He was joined by the rest of them before he reached the ground. Even Lil-Zay reluctantly brought up the rear.

"Y'all bitches chill for a sec!" Dino ordered. Nutty Bar and his newest girl Kit-Kat stopped twerking and followed his eye over to the track.

"Shoot the one then!" Rallo laughed and stepped back.

"Go to the dorm," Trouble told Darius and stepped up and put up them thangs.

"Been wanting to beat that ass!" Bama declared as his put his dukes up as well.

"Bet not nare one of y'all niggas jump!" Gutta announced upon arrival. The Rollers had their knives out so they bared theirs. That set off a chain reaction around the yard and each clique, crew and faction armed themselves.

"Time for a break?" One guard asked the other as all the sharpened steel glinted in the sunlight.

"Fa sho!" She said and lead the way. The inmates could kill each other all they wanted as long as she made it home to her babies.

Bama set it off with a duo of wild haymakers. Trouble smiled at both of them as he dipped and ducked them. He quickly fired off a two piece that busted Bama's thick lips. The Riders all 'oohed' while the Rollers 'aahed'.

"Thought you could fight!" Rallo chided and caused Bama to eat another two piece when he glanced his way.

"Beat that nigga!" Zay cheered from the side. He was more than happy to see the boss put in some work.

"Oh, I'm, finna, beat this, nigga!" Trouble assured him while delivering a blow per word. By the end of the sentence Bama was teetering like a drunk at closing time. Trouble reared back to rock the baby to sleep with a nasty uppercut. "Night-night nigga!"

"Shit!" The witnesses grimaced when Bama's head almost came off like a 'Rock-em sock-em robot.

"Aye, that nigga wasn't no real Roller anyway!" Rallo announced to distance his crew from the sleeping man. He stepped over him while a few stepped on top of him as they left him sleeping in the grass.

A grateful Darius awaited when Trouble finally made it back to the dorm. He was still shaking from the ordeal when he walked in. His lips quivered so much they impeded his speech.

"Th,th, thank, I, I, th, they..." He stammered incoherently. His brain knew the words he wanted to say but had trouble putting them in the proper order.

"Say less. Them niggas some bullies!" Trouble said and ran cold water over his battered knuckles.

"They w,w,w,were g,going to k,k,kill me!" He managed in disbelief.

"Yeah they were. You good now. Fuck with you they fucking with me!" He declared. Fucking with him meant fucking with the Riders.

"I w,won't forget this! On god I'll make this up to you!" he vowed and meant every word. He wasn't a part of the gang but the gang had his back. Only one person really wanted that smoke.

Chapter Fifteen

"*S*o, this the nigger stepping on my toes huh?" Rabbit asked as he watched Trouble. All Ghost heared was 'my' instead of 'ours' and didn't answer.

"That's him," JC replied. It took a while for the White Boys to pinpoint the source of competition since Trouble knew how to cover his tracks. There's plenty of silly niggas wanting to be the man so he let them be the face, while he stacked the dough.

Rabbit had to admit he liked the way the kid moved. He had little to no respect for blacks simply because he had been victimized at an early age. Before that he got along great with every one. Most of the gang bangers were loud and reckless without reason. Trouble was reserved and deliberate. The right traits to make some serious money after he was gone.

"Let's hang his black ass!" Ghost suggested. He was so eager to call shots he had started even before the shot caller left.

"We could? Or we could let him make some money for us?" He posed as a question to question his fitness for the position. He was all about a dollar so if it didn't make cents it didn't make sense.

"White power! We have to let the niggers know this is

MAGA country! Trump is still the president!" He chanted like the truly possessed who followed the man.

"Not yet," Rabbit repeated and looked back towards Trouble. Yeah, he liked the way the kid moved indeed. His gaze travelled until it fell upon the Bandos. One Eyed Dino had his hoes twerking but was looking off into the distance. The monster had been awfully introspective lately. Like he had a lot on his mind.

~

"CLAYTON, DETAIL!" THE DORM OFFICER ANNOUNCED THROUGH the speaker.

"I heard it!" Trouble yelled before the repeaters got a chance to repeat it. He regretted it instantly when he saw how disappointed they looked. People do their time differently, and you have to let them.

"I should go to church?" Darius asked as Trouble got ready for detail.

"Uh, no you shouldn't," he laughed and shook his head vigorously. He had never been to church on the street that he could recall, but was pretty sure they didn't do any of the things he had witnessed.

"I think I'll take your word for it," he decided and accepted the phone. Darius could have bought his own but with Trouble always at detail, visit or yard he didn't need to.

"Good idea," he said and stepped from the cell. There was just enough time to swing by the kitchen and get a few pounds of pussy before work. Trouble pulled rank and bypassed the line to her tonsils since the hot, bubbly box was reserved for him.

"Hey Trouble," Jessie cooed like a school girl with a crush. She actually sounded like Bama when Dino came calling.

"Hey yaself," he greeted as they prepared for a quick quickie. She had that microwave pussy that got super hot and got the job done in a few minutes.

"Your friend dropped off some more of your stuff," she said as she came out of her big girl pants and big girl panties.

"Pablo, yeah," he said since he knew that already.

"Mmhm, and his girlfriend. She had to pee so she came in. Pregnant girls pee a lot I hear," she said as he lined his erection in front of her juicy box.

"This, don't, make no, damn, sense!" He proclaimed as he pushed inside the tight space. He lifted her gut and dipped under it for a good stroke.

"Dang! Dang! Dang! Damn!" She grunted along with each thrust. She certainly couldn't complain about him coming so quickly since she always came quicker. A few more thrusts and she shivered and shook. That already tight vagina convulsed and caused Trouble to explode inside of her.

"Don't, make, no damn, sense!" He repeated as he skeeted inside of her. Putting her on the pill and reserving the pussy for himself allowed him to hit it raw and not have to pull out.

"Here you go daddy," Jessie said as she reached for a rag. As soon as he pulled out her squishy box she was right there to clean and dry him off.

"Let me go to work before Chap fire my ass," he laughed and pulled his pants up. He was joking of course since Chaplain Gayle loved the polite young man. His manners had even improved from the good influence of his bunk-mate. He was one foot out the door when a thought twisted his handsome face.

"What's wrong baby?" Jessie asked when he turned around with the puzzled look.

"What was her name? What did she look like?" He wondered. "The pregnant girl, who had to pee."

"Pretty, dark lil thing with a round belly!" She smiled happy an demonstrated her round her belly was with her hand.

"Her name tho!" He snapped harsher than he intended and cleaned it up. "My bad baby. What was her name?"

"Malaysia. Same place you finna take me with all that money I'm holding for you!" She said and popped a kiss on his agape lips. He was so drunk from the revelation it didn't dawn on him that she kissed him with them same lips that sucked dicks all day, five days a week.

~

"WHAT'S WRONG WITH YOU SON?" NEW YORK ASKED WITH worry in his tone when Trouble arrived at work. He had been in the Chaplain's detail long enough to know that look. It was the same look men had after receiving notice of a loved ones death. Some long term vets had to endure it time and time again as every one they know and love dies off one by one.

"Huh?" He asked since nothing made sense to him at the moment. He tried to make sense of it too but nothing yet.

There were just so many women in Atlanta. Because it's, well it's Atlanta. Baddie central, second only to New York City. Atlanta has a higher female to male ratio because so many dudes like dudes. It just made no sense. Why would Pablo fuck his girl out of all the girls in the world.

"You, OK. Are you?" New York asked in makeshift sign language. It wasn't really sign language but it wouldn't matter since Trouble didn't know sign language either.

"Naw, not really," he admitted but wouldn't elaborate. Not that the New Yorker could help since he has women issues of his own.

"Good evening gentlemen," Chaplain greeted happily. Her smile dissipated when she registered the pain on the young man's face. "You OK? Need a squirt of anointing oil? Get yourself straight before service?"

"Nah, I'm good!" Trouble said and got a good laugh. It was just the medicine he needed to feel a little better. Now all he had to do was curse Malaysia out one good time and he would heal.

"Well, let's get ready to spread the good news!" She cheered and walked off humming a Supreme's tune.

The night moved extra slow for New York since Lalonda was working tonight. She said she had something special for him and he just knew it would be on one of her mama's biscuits. Not to mention a dose of that good southern pussy New Yorkers flock south for. The weather is a plus but that down south booty is the real attraction.

"Let me hear you say hooooooo!" Chaplain cheered and the men cheered with her as she wrapped up her sermon.

"Finally!" Trouble muttered since he was ready to rush back and get on the phone. Once the men filed out they put their gloves on to stack up the chairs since some dudes jacked on the old Chaplain as well. She didn't mind since it was better than messing with each other. That's why she squeezed a little oil in every palm when they came in.

"Hell yeah!" New York exclaimed as the last chair went into the stack. Once again he passed his token meal off to Trouble since he has some food waiting back at his housing unit. The two men didn't even say 'goodbye' or 'see you later' before rushing off to handle their perspective business. Lalonda was all smiles when New York arrived.

"Hey inmate, I need you to sweep and mop this hall," she said and pointed around for anyone looking. This is prison and someone is always looking.

"Yes ma'am," he nodded and followed her to the mop closet. He looked down at her fat booty in the uniform pants and felt his dick throb. They mutually attacked each other as soon as they stepped inside. New York and Lalonda made out hot and heavy while groping each others body. They felt all they could feel through the clothes before stepping back to strip.

"Take your foot all the way out!" He ordered since he wanted to really get to it tonight.

"OK," she agreed and did what she was told. But first she had a surprise for him and rushed to do it before she lost her nerve.

"Oh word?" He cheered when she dipped low and took the dick into her mouth. His knees buckled and he almost lost his balance. Lalonda had brushed up on a series of dick sucking techniques and tried them all. The medley of her mouth had him squirming and moaning. Lalonda knew what that meant from the videos and wasn't ready for all that. She sucked him right to the brink and snatched him out of her mouth with split second to spare.

"Fuck!" He grunted and sent an arch of unwanted children flying over her shoulder. He had plans on eating more than just mama's biscuits himself so he slid between her thick thighs. The fresh smell of her clean vagina greeted him like aloha dancers when you land in Honolulu.

"Dang!" She proclaimed when he got to sucking on her juicy box like a fresh mango. And just like a fresh mango it sent juice flowing all down his chin. They say one good turn deserves another but the same applies for nuts. New York threw his tongue into overdrive when she began to writhe beneath his mouth.

"Mmhm!" He hummed knowingly when she started to shiver and quiver. A gush of nectar filled his mouth when she came with a guttural growl. He scrambled to get the dick in her while she was still pulsating and convulsing. The plan was to really beat the box up but the box had it's own agenda. Lalonda was at such a heightened sexual state she came again in just a few strokes. That tight vagina contracted and convulsed causing him to come right along with her.

"Shit!" They both cussed because good sex elicits bad words.

"I can't wait until you get out so we can just lay here and fall asleep in each others arms!" She sighed as they instead stood and rushed to get dressed.

"Uh, yeah..." He said since that would be nice. He only had a few weeks left to go before his debt to this state was paid.

"Don't forget this!" She sang and came out with one of her mama's biscuits.

"Thanks babe," he sighed. "Fuck them floors tho."

"Fuck em!" She agreed and let him back into his dorm to shower, eat and prepare for another day in the chain gang.

Chapter Sixteen

"*Y*ou better go 'head and answer it," Pablo sighed since the phone kept ringing. It rang all night until Malaysia finally turned it off. Now again the second she turned it back on.

"Do I have toooooo!" She moaned and gripped his dick. Pablo had spent the night here sleeping in the California king that Trouble bought.

"That's yo baby daddy," he reminded. They shared a human so they still had to maintain ties.

"Oh, OK," she pouted and kissed her way down to his stomach before taking the call. "Hello?"

"Hello? Fuck you mean, hello? Like you don't know who the fuck calling?" Trouble snapped despite swearing he wasn't going to snap. That was last night though and he had been calling since then.

"I'll just slide out the way here..." Darius said and left to give him some privacy.

"I know who you are, Trouble," she sassed and added an exclamation by kissing Pablo's dick. He just shook his head at the treachery.

"So why you? How come you?" He began but cut short from asking questions he had no business asking. Especially the ones he already knew the answers to. "So, I hear you got a new man?"

"And you got a new bitch!" She shot back. She had been genuinely heart broken when she found out about Jessie. He could say he took one for the team but so could she. "Look, we cousins anyway. That's not right. I hate you even talked me into this."

"Talked you, you the one, I was..." He stammered as he vividly recalled the night she slid into his room and bed. She used the free time to take Pablo into her mouth. He was now rock hard again despite having sex all night. Pregnant pussy is the best so he spent the night in it.

"Look, we got a son. I'm gonna take care of him. Granny branging him down to see you. You know I would never keep you from him, but," she laid out and paused to lick the throbbing dick in her hand.

"But what?" He wondered, knowing she wasn't about to say what he thought she was about to say.

"You cain't keep calling me. We don't like it," she said and took him back into her mouth.

"That's what's up. Just make sure my son straight! Make sure my bread straight! We don't never gotta talk!" He snapped and she agreed by hanging up the call. Trouble paced the small cell hotly before deciding to make another call. He had the number programmed into the phone so all it took was the press of a button.

"Hole up for a sec, it's him," Pablo warned since Malaysia was engaged in a whole blow job by now.

"Mm-mm," she declined and shook her head with a mouthful of dick. Pablo shrugged and took the call anyway.

"Sup shawty! I know y'all ain't ready for some more work already!" He greeted and went straight to business. They were making far too much money to fall out over a chick. They were doing good business and he was even holding tens of thousands of dollars for him. It went up every time he made another drop.

"Huh? Almost," Trouble said, sidetracked by the business.

He shook it off and got to what he was calling about. "You fucking my girl?"

"Naw bruh, ssss, un-uh," he said and grimaced as she gagged down below.

"Bruh, we bigger than that now!" Trouble said with warning in his tone. "You gonna tell me, you not fucking Malaysia?"

"Malaysia yeah, but she not yo girl. I fucks with you the long way, but she with me now," he said. Malaysia was so happy to hear him claim her she gagged again on the dick and threw her wrist into overdrive.

"Bruh, you, we, um..." Trouble searched for words but found none. He clicked off seconds before being scarred with the sounds of Pablo skeeting down her throat.

"You good bruh?" Darius asked when he returned to see the faraway look in his eyes. The pain was evident but prison was pain on a daily basis.

"Huh? Hell yeah!" He said and snapped out of it. Darius often told him about the women in his world. They owned homes and businesses. Took trips and vacations. He wanted one of those. That meant leaving the hood rats in the hood.

~

"Say cuz!" Rallo greeted way too excited. He was hyped up off the meth and gossip when he saw his cousin in the dorm.

"Sup Rallo?" Trouble replied in that tone people use when their not with the shits at the moment.

"I heard about cuz. She foul!" He said almost sounding sincere except for the smirk. "Yo own partner tho?"

"Shit I ain't mad tho. We still getting money!" He shot back in his own defense.

"You and Pablo?" He asked greedily. Word was spreading that the Riders were eating good off the meth trade and he wanted in.

"Hell yeah, fuck them white boys!" He bragged just to

shine on his cousin. Trouble was a good person at heart and good people can't think the way bad people do.

"Facts! You my role model cuz. Real spit, I like how you rock. Fuck a bitch, get money!" Rallo proclaimed even though said bitch was his cousin. It took a big man to overlook the dis and focus on the money. Rallo wasn't big nor really a man so he started scheming on a come up.

Trouble walked away feeling real smug after flaunting in front of Rallo's broke ass. He forgot the man was a snake and always on the fuck shit. Reecie was the one who told him about Malaysia and Pablo so he got her back on the line to find out what else she knew. He still called shots on the streets with the Rollers who were eager to do his bidding and get props. Most props are really just propaganda and that ain't worth shit.

"Boy I know you ain't tryna see no pussy again!" Reecie fussed when she took the call. She was fussing but coming out of her panties at the same time. She wasn't quite sure who this baby daddy was but Rallo still shot her some bread from time to time.

"Shit, may as well," he agreed even if that wasn't what he called for. They switched to video chat so they could get freaky. That plump, pregnant pussy did look pretty good so he didn't mind a few more pics and videos. Plus he rented the pics and videos out for people to jack off to.

"Let me see something too!" She cheered as she bust it open for him. Rallo complied and squirted a little of Chaplain Gayle's so-called anointed oil. No one needed to know it actually came from the dollar store. It was good and slick, perfect for jacking.

"Here go this dick!" He said and aimed as he pulled. She played in her pussy until he grunted and bust on the floor. Rallo was a Viking too and wasn't going to clean it up.

"Dang!" Reecie cheered since she liked to watch men skeet. She usually didn't get to see it since they were usually in her mouth or vagina.

"I know, right," he panted since a good nut can take the

breath away. "Say, what that nigga Pablo be driving these days? Still got that Lexus?"

"Hell naw! He got a bad ass Benz! Black with black guts, moon roof..." She said until he could pick the car out anywhere.

"He be spinning a night at Lay-lay place?" He slid in next since she was talking.

"Mmhm. All the time!" She pouted since it cut down on her visits when he was there. "You finna send me some money?"

"Hell yeah," he agreed and sent a cash app on the spot. She certainly earned it.

Chapter Seventeen

"*E*xcuse me sir? Mr Sa'id," Sa'id heard as he scoured the law book in front of him.

"Yes!" He said harsher than intended since court was coming up and he was brushing up on his arguments.

"They call me Bama, but I wanna be a moozlim now," Bama announced. He had been all over looking for him since getting knocked out on the yard.

"Aren't you the one who got knocked out on the yard?" Sa'id recalled.

"Huh? Oh, yeah. I had weaved but I was supposed to duck. I 'shoulda dipped and came up with a..." He demonstrated until getting cut off.

"Wasn't you a Rider, then a Roller and now you wanna be a Muslim?" He asked trying to make it make sense. This wasn't the NBA where you can just switch teams. Islam is a whole way of life, not just changing jerseys. It was also common knowledge that he snitched on his own people. None of which preclude a person from embracing Islam when they genuinely want to change their lives. Unfortunately most don't and are just looking for safety in numbers. If they only knew it was Allah who protected them, not their numbers.

"Un-uh. Yeah," he nodded. "I needs to get down with someone. You feel me?"

"You good akh?" Samir came over and asked when he saw Sa'id's face change.

"Naw, cuz this nigga is still talking to me!" He snapped. Being disturbed from his law work was bad enough but another person trying to make a mockery of his way of life was even worse.

"Beat it before you get some knots on your head!" Samir advised and balled his fist in case he wanted those knots.

"Some more knots you mean!" Sa'id laughed since Trouble had left a few. "One of them look like a may not."

"A May Knot?" Samir asked since he was unfamiliar with the term.

"A may not, as in it may not go away!" He laughed and turned back to his book. Samir just shook his head and walked off. Sa'id may write some funny shit in a book but is real corny in person. A regular nerd, but sincere about his religion.

Bama got put on the door after getting knocked out on the yard. None of the Rollers wanted him around and he was a wanted man with the Riders. Lil-Zay vowed to murder him on sight and he had no doubt he would do it.

There was only one dorm without Rollers or Riders that he could go to. It had White boys, who wouldn't have him. Nor would the Mexicans even though he tried to pretend he was from Panama. The Muslims told him he had to talk to Sa'id and that didn't turn out well. There was only one group left and their leader had his eyes on Bama the moment he moved in. Well, eye that is.

"Sup bruh. Tryna smoke one?" Dino asked as he pushed up on the man without a country. Nutty Bar, Honey Bun and Cupcake all pretended to watch TV while their daddy did his thing.

"Shit, I really could use a joint, but I ain't with the fuck shit!" He said when he should have said no. Just a plain old no, and mind his business.

"Ain't no fuck shit. Come on," Dino said over his shoulder and headed to his cell. Bama looked around for other options but found none. He really did want to get high so he got up and followed him inside the room.

The dorm was relatively quiet as the men went through their daily routines. The Mexicans cooked a big meal to share while the White boys shot methamphetamine in their veins. The Muslims and Christians each held down a table for their studies. The Bandos waited for the weed and homemade wine to do what it does before they got up and eased into the cell.

Anyone who has ever heard a man being raped will tell you it never goes away. The howl of penetration penetrates to the bone marrow. It's a mix of pain, fear and shock that made Bama sober instantly.

"Akh?" Malik said and stood. He couldn't sit by and listen and not act.

"Bruh we told him, we tell err body!" Musa reminded. They made it their business to warn every new person who moved in what Dino and the Bandos were about. They did so right in his face in case he didn't like it. He didn't but liked it better than dying so it was what is was. And why wouldn't it be when dudes still put themselves in that position.

And when they do Dino put them in another position. 'The buck' and raped them face to face so they could see what was happening. Bama put up a fight for his booty but not a good enough fight and got raped.

Bama walked in that cell a man but came out a girl. His new name was Swiss Miss since hot chocolate was already taken.

∾

"WE FINNA HANDLE THIS TODAY!" SHAKUR GROWLED AS HE AND Sa'id made their way to Friday prayer. It technically wasn't Sa'id's week to give the khutbah but the recent revelations changed everything. Some religions have gay pastors but Islam is not one of them.

"Yeah we do," Sa'id agreed with a heavy heart. He had hoped things would have went better so he could chill, but sometimes you have to step up.

Word that Jahil likes boys had spread with the ferocious-ness of a out west wildfire. The sanctity of the whole community was thrown off by the wicked deeds of the prayer leader. The Muslim's respect and honor was on the line.

The Friday prayer is held in the same room as visitation on the weekend. It could easily hold the hundreds of men who came to pray heel to heel, shoulder to shoulder. Most times the men would make some voluntary prayer upon arrival and sit quietly reflecting upon the greatness of God until the Imam comes out to give the sermon known as a khutbah.

That's most Fridays. This Friday everyone was standing and in two distinct groups. Jahil and more than half of them stood on one side while the others stood on the other. The moment of truth was here and people picked a side.

Some were with the bullshit and wanted to sell drugs, fuck with boys, not pray or do anything that Islam is. Abandoning the five daily prayers removes a person from the fold of Islam in itself. Jahil and the hundred or so men with him didn't combine to make five prayers in day.

The other side wasn't perfect but they were trying. Some had some of the same issues as the other side but had the sincerity to keep striving. The Muslim has a self reproaching soul. When they do good they are pleased. When they fall short they feel bad and repent.

Jahil and his crew possessed the soul that commands evil. Some of them didn't have any good in them. Others were still slaves to their desires and no man can serve two masters. The door of rectitude and repentance is always open, but for now they chose a side.

Sa'id couldn't help but remember when he once would have been on that side. Not because of the disbelief, but disobedience. Everyone will certainly go from stage to stage in life. He was no longer in that one.

"We may as well get straight to the shit!" Jahil demanded once everyone was present.

"OK, first of all, this is yawma jumu'ah. Friday prayer. Watch yo mouth!" Shakur snapped. That could have been the spark that lit the fuse but Sa'id chimed in to calm things down.

"First, as salaamu alaykum. Like the brother said, this our special day. We're going to respect it," he said and nodded.

Nodding is like a Jedi mind trick and makes people nod along with it. "Now, you know what's been said..."

"I said it! I seen it!" Fuck-Shit spoke up and dared him to deny it. Not that he could since he'd been doing it for years and people turned a blind eye since he had the drugs.

"It is what it is. I'm still the Imam! I still run the Muslims!" He dared.

"I was hoping for a peaceful transfer of power but, whatever..." Sa'id shrugged and moved forward. Those loyal to Allah and his messenger moved with him. Jahil and his crew moved forward except a few.

"Hole up bruh. I ain't with this shit!" Jahil's right hand man suddenly decided and pulled his kufi off.

"Fuck you doing bruh!" He pleaded to keep the man at his side.

"Bruh we don't even believe what they believe! We talked about this shit before. Let them folks have they religion," he said as Sa'id and the striving Muslims closed in. Dying for the sake of Allah is an honorable death and each one was with it. Whoever would die for a cause will kill for it and they were with that too.

"He right," another said and removed his kufi as well. One by one they all walked off and left Jahil standing by himself. Most left all together, some switched sides in favor of changing their lives for the better.

They came with every intention of killing Jahil and whoever wanted to die with him. He stuck his chest out and pulled a knife to fight. There would be no fighting today though because Sa'id simply turned away and took position to deliver the khutbah.

*"Authoo billahi minash shaitonir rajeem. Bismillahir Rahmanir Raheem. Innal hamdulillahi Rabbil alameen...*We begin by seeking refuge with Allah from the rejected devil. Then with the name of Allah, the help of Allah and the blessings of Allah....

Allah revealed in the Qur'an, you are the best of peoples raised from mankind. Because you enjoin the good, forbid the evil and believe in Allah. Dear brothers, that is our whole religion...."

Sa'id gave the khutbah not knowing it would be his last. He was summoned to court the next week and granted relief. He received credit for time served and was released. Probably never to be heard from again...

~

"HEY RABBIT, THEY'RE CALLING FOR YOU!" ONE OF THE White boys announced as Rabbit's government name was called through the intercom.

"You don't think he fucking hears it? You fucking, fuck!" Ghost snapped.

"Fucking sorry ass fucking counselor. With her sorry ass!" Rabbit groaned as he got ready to go out. He knew he had an appointment but deliberately dragged since his counselor was sorry as fuck.

After putting his state clothes on he made his way through the dorm and out the door. He returned white power salutes all the way to the counselor's office, where the sorry ass counselors sat on their sorry asses.

"Excuse me," A drunken Fitz staggered by. He bumped right into Rabbit without even looking up to see who he bumped into. He was also coming out of the sorry ass counselor's office.

"Must have socked it to him," Rabbit said and assumed the same. Parole letters had been coming in and that's rarely good news. A long enough set off can make a man drunk just like Fitz.

"Hey Johnson. She waiting on you," the inmate clerk advised and opened the door. Rabbit wore a snarl as he went in and found his counselor sitting on her sorry ass, not doing shit.

"Parole letter," she said and handed it across the desk. She already knew what it said and watched his face for a reaction. His eyes scanned the few lines, then went back to the top an read them again.

"What does this mean, exactly?" Rabbit had to ask since he just couldn't make sense of it on his own.

"That means you've been granted parole. Stay out of trouble and you'll be home in a few months," she said and looked behind him for her clerk. "Next man!"

Rabbit was just as drunk as Fitz had been since he just received the same news. It was his turn to stumble drunk into the next man.

"My bad," he managed to say without even looking up. He moved around the man and kept on pushing.

"No problems lil mama," Dino laughed as he watched his ass. "Let me see what this sorry ass counselor want."

Dino was the next man to stumbled drunkenly from the counselors office. He too had made parole.

Chapter Eighteen

"*S*hawty a bad lil bitch!" Lil-Zay laughed and pointed at Bama. He and Nutty Bar were twerking in tiny shorts for Dino but his one eye was elsewhere.

Dino, Rabbit and Fitz had all received the news lifers wait a life for, parole. The state played the game of giving the good news, then making them wait months for it to manifest. Some fucked up in the interim, proving they weren't ready to go home.

Sometimes they denied parole just to see how an inmate will react to the bad news. Life is filled with bad news and set backs. If they nutted up they just proved they weren't ready to go home. If they stayed calm and stayed the course they would come back a couple months later and grant parole.

"Knew he was a bitch," Trouble laughed. Snitches are bitches, that's why they rhyme.

Bama pouted when he saw his old friends watching him as he worked it. He could have been with them, kicking it and smoking weed if he kept it a hundred. Instead he was twerking and getting smashed by One Eyed Dino. They saw someone approaching from the rear and spun to address them.

"What's up my nigga?" Lil-Zay barked and stuck his chest out. The same concept of the puffer fish since a knife appeared in each hand.

"We didn't come for that," Rabbit said calmly. Ghost moved his hands closer to his own knives since he was eager to go to war.

"Well, what did you come for?" Trouble asked. He had a clue since his income going up meant he was inching into the White boys meth market.

"To talk business. Let these two play while we spin one?" He offered and nodded towards the track.

"Play nice," Trouble chuckled towards Zay and fell instep with Rabbit. Lil-Zay and Ghost just glared at each other as their bosses talked business.

Lil-Zay was a goon and only wanted to do goon shit. Plus he was high off meth so he wanted to go to war with someone. Anyone as long as he could stab someone. Ghost wanted war too but right now he was pouting about being left out of another meeting. He was trying to be patient until Rabbit put him in charge but was running out of patience.

"What can I do for you?" Trouble asked rather professionally. A trait he had picked up from Darius that he finally got to try. Rabbit snapped his head in surprise since he took Trouble for a regular street nigga.

"It's more like, what I can do for you," he corrected and added. "Make you rich!"

"I ain't far from that now!" He shot back since he was up a couple hundred grand already. Not exactly rich but definitely in the right direction.

"Probably," Rabbit nodded since he had been slinging meth in the chain gang long enough to know. He had a cool half a million waiting for him to come spend. "But, why spend money on re-ups? Why not get a drop every week and supply the whole compound?"

"You mean the nigga part of the compound don't you?" Trouble clarified since the White boys had most of giving the camp on smash.

"No!" He said and turned to face him. "Fuck them crackers! Fuck that white power bullshit! I wanna make money!"

"I'm listening..." Trouble said and did just that as Rabbit explained how he would leave the mule to him instead of

Ghost. He had been doing this long enough to read the deceit and treachery in his eyes.

∼

"As salaamu alaykum akhi. What the fuck?" Samir asked Shakur. "You see this shit?"

"I see it," he said as he looked over at the group of Rollers. It looked like it had doubled since absorbing most of the renegade ex-muslims, if there is such a thing. About sixty of the renegades joined the Rollers so they could be in on the bullshit. Rallo condoned the fuck shit which was right up their alley.

He gave Jahil his own sect since he brought more manpower into the fold. Some of the renegades went over to the Riders if they had cousins or homeboys in the gang. A few just chose Trouble over Rallo. The effect was immediate and the Rollers roamed the yard getting into fights and taking people's property.

"Did Fu...uh, Raheem come out?" Shakur asked and scanned the yard for the teen. Jahil vowed to do something to him for exposing him.

"Nah, he short as gorilla glue girl's hair. He staying in," Samir before the old man took off running. A few more brothers fell instep and followed them both back inside.

Jahil and three more Rollers were seen leaving Fuck-Shit's dorm as they neared. They ignored them and rushed inside to check on the young brother. The mood in the dorm spoke before they reached his cell. Violence leaves a stain on faces and souls that last longer than the blood stains on the concrete floors.

"Subhanillah!" Shakur croaked when he saw Fuck-Shit stretched out in a pool of his own blood. "Get help!"

One of the brothers ran back to the booth to summon the officer. He pretended not to know what was going on even though he let Jahil and the others inside the dorm. Quite of few of the younger male officers were infatuated with the gang bangers and did favors for them. Others actually joined the gangs on the street before they started working in the prison.

"What's up?" The officer asked.

"We need medical! Get help!" He shouted.

"What's wrong?" The officers asked to draw it out long enough for Fuck-Shit to bleed out.

"Fuck him!" Another brother decided when he peeped what he was doing since he'd seen it before. "Somebody gimme a phone!"

"Here," someone said and discretely slid him a phone. He called 9-11 from the prison dorm while Shakur and the others applied pressure and carried him out to the yard.

"Clear the yard! Everyone back to the dorms!" The officers shouted once they got word that the helicopter was on the way. Shakur and Jahil locked eyes as they passed each other once again. Both cracked sinister smiles but for different reasons.

Jahil was happy to get some get back at being exposed as a fuck boy. Meanwhile, Shakur was a Muslim for real and the religion allows retribution. An eye for and eye, wounds equal for equal. Jahil was going to get stabbed the fuck up just like Fuck-Shit. If the kid died, he would too.

~

"FUCK! SHIT! FUCK!" PABLO GRUNTED AND GROANED AS HE dug Malaysia out from the back so he wouldn't lay on her baby bump. Plus, it was super good like that with the added sensation of watching himself slide in and out of her creamy box.

"Uhnnnnn nigga!" She grunted and squeezed, knowing what it would do.

"Argh!" Pablo grunted and busted a good nut. She clamped down so tight he couldn't have pulled out if he wanted to. Who would want to though. Especially since she couldn't get any more pregnant than she was right now.

"Who dick, is, this!" She teased and squeezed. Then cracked up as he squirmed and moaned.

"That shit don't make no damn sense!" He cheered and clapped for the pussy. A bomb shot of pussy does deserve a round of applause.

"Mmhm, remember this, good-good, when you out there handling yo biznizz!" She said with a final squeeze before releasing her grip.

"How could I ever forget it?" He asked honestly. It really takes a special kind of male to chase random pussy when they have some good pussy at home.

"Mmhm," she hummed happily as he went into the bathroom to wash his dick in the sink. He slipped into his clothes and popped a kiss on her forehead before stepping back through the living room.

"Hey," Reecie greeted from the sofa like she wasn't just listening to them fuck through the door.

"Hey," he sighed and kept it moving. Pablo got into his Benz and began a series of calls to set up a series of stops. Being a mid level dope dealer meant dropping off dope and picking up money.

He saw a dark sedan pull out after him but didn't register it. Several stops later he noticed it again but his phone distracted him. His head shook when he saw Malaysia's tight box on his screen. It couldn't be ignored so he took the call.

"Yoo," Pablo said and relaxed a little when the car took a left turn when he made a right.

"Pick me up some S&S while you out?" She asked but didn't need to wait for an answer since he never told her 'no' to anything. "Pecan waffle with the Nashville hot chicken please!"

"And this dick is dessert," he said and committed the order to memory.

"Mmmm, all that cream!" She teased and licked her lips.

"Hole up. Yo other baby daddy calling," he said when Trouble's number appeared on the screen.

"Handle yo biz," she said and twisted her lips like Trouble did her wrong. She just happened to be one of those selfish ass people who do you wrong and beat you getting mad. Forgiveness kills them folks. She knew he and Trouble were still getting money and wouldn't interfere with that. Especially since she was spending it as fast as it came in.

"Sup bruh?" Pablo said and braced himself to see which way the call would go. Trouble cut their last call short but that was personal, this was business.

"You my nigga," he shot back, sounding like he did before the recent revelation. "What we looking like?"

"Like rock stars! This shit booming shawty! I'm finna shoot down tomorrow and hit yo girl off," he said since it was time to resupply big Jessie with work.

"That's what the fuck I'm talmbout!" Trouble cheered as well. They were making plenty of money already but he would accept Rabbit's offer and make even more. "Say, about that other thang..."

"I know bruh, I..." Pablo began but Trouble cut in before he could finish.

"It's all good bruh. It fucked me up at first but, I'm good. She a good chick. You a good dude. Make sure my shawty is straight, but he bet not call you daddy!" He got out just like he had practiced.

"Never that!" Pablo assured him. He was about to be a dad himself and couldn't imagine his child calling the next man daddy. They laughed it up while that same sedan pulled around the corner and fell in behind him.

"A'ight my nigga. I'll hit you when I get down y'all way tomorrow," Pablo said when Malaysia popped back on the line.

"Check," he agreed and clicked off.

"Feel better?" Darius asked once Trouble hung up.

"I do. I really do," he nodded. He may have but Pablo was about to feel something else.

"What he want? He still mad? What he say about me?" Malaysia rambled as Pablo took her call and came to a stop at a red light.

"He said..." Pablo was saying until the same sedan whipped up beside him. The three passengers hopped out and pointed four guns between them.

"Run that shit!" One holding two pistols shouted from the front while two others holding AR/15s stood on both sides.

"What's going on!" Malaysia screamed but she was going to need to scream louder to be heard over all the shooting. Because Pablo panicked and turned a regular robbery into a homicide.

Pablo tossed the car into reverse and stomped on the gas pedal. The man in front tugged each trigger and riddled the windshield with forty caliber slugs. Both men on both sides let the choppers rip. Pablo did the Atl version of the Harlem shake as slugs tore into from each angle. An early head shot spared him from feeling any of the other bullets that entered his body.

"Pablo! Baby! Pablo!" Malaysia shouted in horror as the barrage of gunfire stopped as suddenly as it erupted. Pablo couldn't hear her from where he was at.

"Get the work!" The driver shouted since his focused hadn't changed.

The shooter in front tucked his tools and opened the front door. He ignored the sight and smell of blood as he rummaged through the dead mans pockets. Another popped the trunk and made off with a satchel of money. They hopped back in and chirped off. A few blocks away the driver made a call.

"Y'all get him?" Rallo wanted to know when he took that call. They had kept him informed as they trailed him all week and finally made their move.

"Hell yeah we did! Got bread and work!" He cheered. They did strike for thirty grand in cash and another twenty in drugs. Nothing compared to if they had followed him home where nearly half a million in drugs, and cash were stashed.

Chapter Nineteen

"*How* ow is he?" Shakur asked and held his breath. Good character allowed him to keep a good relationship with the staff which allowed him to get good information on the patient.

"Not good," the nurse sighed and shook her head. Shakur nodded and turned to go kill Jahil but she spoke up again before he did. "He'll live. Lost a lot of blood, but he'll live."

"In sha Allah," the old man sighed since it meant Jahil might live too. He was still getting stabbed so it would be God's will if he lived or died. The kid got hit twenty nine times which means they took it easy on him. Many hits run fifty licks or better. Jahil wasn't the only one getting stabbed though since the other three Rollers were identified as well. The Rollers had the numbers at the moment but that didn't mean they got a pass. The Muslims would get their vengeance and whatever happens will just happen.

"Look at this kafir!" Samir growled and turned his phone to Shakur when he got back to the dorm.

"I don't no nothing about this book face, telegram, instant gram..." The old man fussed.

"Um, it's instagram, but look at the face. That's ole boy!" He corrected. That required Shakur to put his glasses on if he was going to see something. Which is why he usually kept them off since there was too many things he'd rather not see. There was always someone pulling on their dick since going without pussy is part of the punishment. That was bad but worse was men hugging, kissing and holding hands.

"That's, uh, Vinson? Officer Vinson!" He exclaimed when he saw the same officer who let Rollers into the dorm to stab Fuck-Shit nearly to death.

"Yeah, that's him. With his dumb ass!" Samir acknowledged. He added the 'dumb ass' because his dumb ass was in front of his own house. The house number was clearly visible in the picture. He tilted his head at the elder to ask a question. A slight nod was the tacit answer, since all it took is a nod to get your dumb ass killed.

"Jahil is mine. Ion care about the rest," Shakur said and walked off so he couldn't hear Samir do what needed to be done.

For some odd reason some dirty officers do dirty shit to inmates and don't think about it coming back. Like they didn't leave families and loved ones behind. Or goons who didn't mind driving to put some work in. Samir was from Savannah. The pretty city by the ocean, full of goons. They took the call and answered the call. Officer Vinson's timeline was going to look real different, real soon.

~

"SHIT FINNA HIT THE FAN!" TROUBLE SIGHED WHEN HE GOT off the phone.

"Can it get any worse?" Darius asked in disbelief. The prison had went from bad to worse as soon as the Rollers numbers increased. That translated to a few more in each dorm and that in turn translated to more fuck shit. The young gang bangers were hyped up on meth and running wild.

"It will be if this officer gets wacked!" he said and began putting his contraband away.

"An officer? Which officer?" Darius asked urgently. Trouble filled him in on the stabbing and retribution sure to follow. Samir made the mistake of speaking in front of his

124

bunk-mate who told one person and that started an avalanche. News of the hit seeped throughout the prison so people could prepare for the aftermath. The state would crash their party like a ton of bricks if an officer got killed.

"That's not good! Can I make a call before you put up?" he asked.

"Yeah, but hurry," Trouble replied and tossed him the phone. He gathered up his dope and other contraband to be put away. Darius made a quick call to handle his own business. The phone buzzed the second Trouble got it back in his hand. "Shit!" he sighed and twisted his lips at an old picture of Malaysia's vagina. He made a mental note to change it and delete all the pussy pics and videos in the gallery. No sense looking at the next man's property since he had accepted it for what it was. They still had a son so he took the call. "Sup?"

"I cain't believe you so damn dirty!" Malaysia said in a low hiss that actually shook his soul.

"What, cuz I'm over you? Cuz that nigga can have you? I'm dirty for moving on?" he chuckled and made her even angrier.

"I'll just, uh, yeah..." Darius suggested as he eased out of the cell so they could fuss in peace.

"That's what you call it? They shot that man eighteen times and you call it, moving on?" she growled. Malaysia was a typical, loud hood rat but she was so angry now that she spoke just above a whisper.

"Shot who? What the fuck you talking about?" he frowned and switched to his ear bud so he could go online as they spoke. He saw it before she even said it. The 'RIPs' were rolling in for the beloved Pablo.

"I was on the phone with him when you called last night. I know you did that shit. Just couldn't stand to see me happy. Couldn't stand to see me with the next man," she said shaking her head.

"Look, Ion know why the fuck you think I would do that shit!" he snapped. "First of all, I ain't pressed about no pussy! Second, me and bruh was getting money together! Good money! Fuck I look throwing that away for some pussy!"

"You did that shit nigga. Ole hateful, spiteful ass nigga," she snarled. "On god I'ma get you for this shit!"

"On my son..." Trouble began but found himself alone on the line. He tried to call back but it went straight to voicemail. A few calls later the whole number was changed.

"You good?" Darius asked when he returned to find Trouble staring off into space.

"Naw. Anything but..." he sighed and got himself back in motion. He knew the prison would be on super maximum security if the officer got hit and he didn't need those problems.

THE TIME DRAGGED FOR MOST OF THE PRISON WHILE THEY found other ways to pass time without cell phones. Most of the smart ones put their contraband far away before the shit hit the fan. Given advance notice the police weren't finding shit.

That same time passed by quickly for Trouble and Darius. The latter had taught the former how to play chess and Trouble couldn't get enough of it. He didn't know any of the standard openings but had a knack for picking things up. He would probably never beat his teacher but he did pick his brain for other business ideas.

Trouble had a hard time concentrating on the game with the murder of Pablo weighing heavy on his mind. Not that he hadn't thought about it himself a time or two, or three. In the end it was MOB, and he chose money of bitches.

"Especially that bitch!" He grunted at the thought of Malaysia's tight vagina squeezing the next man's dick.

"Huh?" Darius asked and squinted down at the board to see if he could see what he was talking about.

"Who? Where?" He laughed to make a joke out of. He knew he wanted to cry a few times thinking about Pablo smashing Malaysia. At the end of every day they were making too much money to fall out over something that ultimately wasn't his. As many times as she moaned about it being his pussy it really belonged to her. She could, and obviously would, do whatever she pleased with it.

His head shook woefully and a deep sigh escaped his chest as he tried to figure how much money he just lost. Pablo was sitting on at least fifty thousand for him. When their income increased he kept what he gave Malaysia the same and had Pablo hold the rest. That was probably gone along with the work they had in the streets. He could probably get someone else to bring the dope down to Jessie.

"Hell naw!" He had to laugh at his own idea. Granny would definitely do it if he asked but he wouldn't ask.

"You're mind is obviously elsewhere," Darius said after Troubles next move.

"Why you say that?" He asked, even though it was.

"Check mate," he explained and tilted his king.

"Oh," he admitted as the match was lost. He lost every match but put up more of a fight than this. "Hope this shit blow over soon. I got shit to do!"

"I'm sure it will," Darius assured him confidently. Somehow he knew it would.

RALLO AND OTHER RENEGADES DIDN'T PUT THEIR PHONES OR contraband away. They planned to ball til they fall since they would just rob a civilian for a phone if they lost theirs. It was always good to have hot boys on compound who keep the CERT team busy while everyone else could play by the rules. In other words, there could be no geniuses if not for fools. One such fool was on his phone right now.

"What the fuck going on out there lil cuz!" Rallo demanded like he was upset about the news he was hearing from the streets. Even though he heard it when it happened since he made it happen. What he really wanted to know was what the streets were saying. That's more important than the truth most times.

"Man! Oh man!" Reecie grunted enthusiastically. She was delighted to be the first to spread the news.

"What girl!" He said so she would get to it, so he could see some pussy.

"They done kilt Pablo!" She whispered since Malaysia was in the next room. She was totally distraught but it was slowly morphing to anger. Soon a burning rage would grow and consume everything in its vicinity. Even its host.

"Naw, not Pablo!" He reeled believably. A common trait amongst pieces of shit is, that most are really good actors.

"Mmhm. It was on the news and err thing!" She said which was saying a lot since the city had become so danger-ous. The devil had done his job and people hate people enough to murder them every day. Black people especially hate black people and were in serious danger from each other.

Pablo's was one of many killings in and around the city but managed to make the nightly news due to its sheer brutal-ity. Each AR/15 put thirty rounds into the vehicle. The forty caliber pistol held thirty more in an extended clip that made it look like a leg. The entire car was literally totaled by the bullets.

"Some one 'musta had a personal beef with him," Rallo offered the gossipy girl. She was texting and posting as they spoke and added that to the other theories of conspiracies floating online.

"Mmhm," she agreed and dipped into an even lower whis-per. "Lay-lay think Trouble did it."

"Nuh-uh! Bruh in here with me," he offered, so not to give in so easily.

"Shit! As much shit as I be doing for you!" She shot back since if he could have her ripping and running it wouldn't be hard to have someone come gunning.

"Well, he was fucking his girl," Rallo said and smirked in satisfaction. "Now, let me see that fat pussy before your water break!"

"Knew you was finna say something crazy!" She giggled and turned the phone since she already had it ready for him. He had just got a glimpse of the plump lips, glistening from young girl excitement when one of his Rollers called in. Another young officer who worked at the prison with Vinson.

"Hey shawty, keep that thang hot. I gotta take this!" He said and switched over. "Sup shawty?"

"Look, they just locked up Roller-V!" He said of Officer Vinson's gang name.

"Who?" Rallo asked, wondering who locks up the police.

"Ion know? My daddy work for the sheriff department and he say it's over his pay grade," he answered. Neither connected it to the attack at the prison but that's exactly what it was.

The district attorney got the video of Vinson letting the Rollers in a dorm they didn't belong to stab another inmate. Luckily Fuck-Shit would live so he wouldn't catch a murder charge. Jahil and the other Rollers involved were taking to the hole for thirty days. A stabbing like that is called aggravated assault in the free world. It could cost you twenty years of your life in prison. However if you're already in prison, thirty days in the hole. No wonder niggas keep getting stabbed.

Chapter Twenty

"They said that officer just got locked up!" Lil-Zay announced happily when he burst into Trouble and Darius's cell. He extended a smoldering joint and cup of buck to celebrate.

"I'll give y'all some space," Darius offered and got ghost like the weed smoke was poison.

"Yeah ole lame ass nigga!" Zay called after him.

"Why you stay fucking with bruh?" Trouble asked, shaking his head. His loyalty was torn between the friendships of his past and the friendship of his future. He had no intention of going back to the streets once he was released from prison. Darius was the key to his future.

"Cuz, he a lame ass nigga," he replied.

"Anyway, what they talking about with ole boy?" He asked to change the subject. New friends can be endanger from old friends who feel threatened.

"Shit, I heard he got caught with a pack?" He shrugged since rumors were running wild. Each person added a little with it so the truth got further diluted as it went along.

"Good," Trouble nodded since renegade officers bringing shit in messed with his money. He let out a sigh and commenced with the bad news. "Pablo got hit up last night."

"Dang, he good?" Zay asked as the joint made it back to him.

"He dead," Trouble admitted. He almost felt a tinge of guilt simply because Malaysia wrongly blamed him. He also felt a tinge of satisfaction that Pablo couldn't fuck her anymore.

"Bruh, I bet them fuck ass Rollers had something to do with that shit! Word to Ridell we need to clap back!" He shot back hotly. That required firing up another joint so that's what he did.

"Gotta wait til the truth come all the way out. Niggas go to talking crazy when shit first happen. That's why we gotta wait and ascertain the truth." He explained. He obviously forgot who the fuck he was talking to.

"Ass who?" The dumb dude asked and twisted his face at the new word.

"Ascertain, find out, never mind. We'll chill until we can get to the bottom of it." was his decision.

"You changing big bruh. One of our people kill wacked and you 'talmbout somebody ass. We beefing with them damn Rollers out there but you playing nice with them niggas in here!" He fumed. Lil-Zay just wanted to fight and stab but Trouble wouldn't green-light his bullshit.

"Bruh I," Trouble was saying but he stormed out. A loud thunder crack was heard when he slapped the first civilian he saw.

"What I do?" The man asked, holding his raw cheek.

"Come on over!" Rev called out. The older man led the bible studies for the Christians in the dorm and on the yard. He smoked crack on the street, but was a bible scholar in the joint. No contradiction at all since everyone has demons. Falling victim to desires doesn't make anyone less sincere.

"I ain't even say nothing to him!" The man whined. He was literally old enough to be Lil-Zay's daddy and the kid slapped him.

"We'll pray about it," Rev said and reached for his hands.

"I'm getting tired of praying about shit," Curtis growled and shook his head at how it sounded. "I mean..."

"I know exactly what you mean. We still finna pray about it. For now...." Rev said and took his hand as well. The Rollers were raising more and more hell around the camp. Many of the civilians were Christians so they were easy prey. Even some of the Riders robbed the white and black civilians. As a result their numbers grew by the day. If Rev ever decided to bust a grape, that grape would get busted.

"Sensitive ass niggas! Don't know they ass from ascertain!" Trouble grumbled after Zay stormed off. It was followed by a good giggle since he was feeling good from the weed and homemade alcohol. Plus he had something on the horizon to make him feel even better. "Shit, I'm finna go get me some pussy!"

"Whoa! Where are you going?" Darius asked as he returned to see Trouble staggering out of their cell.

"Finna go get me some pussy!" He repeated and swayed. He had been smoking and drinking less lately so his tolerance was down.

"I don't think you should go anywhere?" Darius offered out of concern.

"I'm good my nigga!" He barked and pressed forward. Some people shouldn't drink since it makes them mean and nasty. Trouble was some people. His face twisted into a snarl as he made his way through the dorm and out the door.

"Sup Clayton," the kitchen officer greeted and let him in. He didn't mind the unauthorized inmates once he started getting a kickback from the operation. Trouble grunted in reply and kept on pushing.

"I'm next," an inmate advised when he arrived at Jessie's station.

"You gonna be the next nigga on a helicopter you keep talking to me," he warned and waited to see if he had something more to say. He didn't since a helicopter ride is nowhere near as fun as a blow job.

"I'm finna jump in line over at Tess spot," he surrendered and rushed away.

"Fuck," the man exiting the office exclaimed as if the

weight of the world had been lifted off of his shoulders. A good blow job has that effect, even if short lived.

"Psssh!" Trouble blew his breath in reply and stared the man down. He didn't what any smoke so he dropped his head and hurried off.

"Hey baby! I ain't expect you!" Jessie sang and clapped when she saw her boo. Them other dicks were strictly business, she loved her some Trouble.

Especially since she replaced Malaysia for the late night phone calls. Most nights they would stay up kicking it about everything. Trouble even bounced some of his business ideas off of her. She approved some and shot down others. She even had a nice piece of her own money to invest with him.

"Cuz you too busy drinking come to know what's going on!" He barked. Jessie was too stunned to reply but knew why he was here when he dropped his pants. His flaccid dick fell out but she knew how to fix those.

"Don't worry," she sang and dipped low. "Mama got you..."

"You ain't none of my mama," he growled as she took him into her mouth. A few seconds later he was rock hard and ready. "Get them big ass drawers off. So I can ascertain that fat pussy!"

"Uh, OK," she said even though she didn't appreciate his tone or selection of words. Still, "it's yo pussy!"

"Shit I'm just another nigga fucking yo fat ass! You a hoe. You sell pussy! It's err body pussy!" He declared as he searched for a stroke. Jessie was in shock at his words and blinked in disbelief. His eyes may have been closed but she stared up at him the whole time. The whole time wasn't a long time before he hissed, grunted, cursed and came. "Fat ass got some good ass pussy!"

"Mmhm," she hummed as he skeeted in her and pulled out. He didn't bother washing or even wiping his dick. He tucked it away wet and walked off. Jessie waited until she was alone and had herself a good cry.

She had been wrestling with her profession lately and to hear it put so bluntly was more than she could bare.

Chapter Twenty-One

"The fuck?" Trouble groaned when he awoke to cannons being fired. It sounded like he was in the middle of Gettysburg but it was just another day in the chain gang.

"Yeah, I bet!" Darius laughed since he knew his friend would awake with a nasty hangover. "Here."

"Thanks," he nodded and accepted the cup of cowboy coffee. It was jet black and super strong. He took a sip and decided, "I'm not drinking any more."

"Yeah, I wouldn't," his bunk-mate agreed. He was the one who had to clean up the throw up and break up several near fights he tried to start.

"Been a rough couple of days," Trouble sighed as he sat completely up. It had been too and he wasn't sure which problem should get his attention first.

Pablo getting killed was a problem on several levels since he was holding money for him as well as being the connect. He almost lost a tear along with the recognition that the money was lost. Stack had warned him that one of the pitfalls of hustling in the chain gang was people hustling you. Prisoners need someone to hold their money and honest folks are hard to find. Wives, sisters, brothers, mothers and grand-mothers have all run off or spent up an inmates money.

Trouble tried to minimize that sad fact by spreading his bread out. Malaysia had about two hundred thousand while Pablo was holding a buck. Jessie was up to fifty thousand dollars she was holding for him as well.

"Well, that's dead," he accepted and said it out loud to help it digest. The hundred thousand Pablo had was gone.

"What's dead?" Darius asked.

"Huh? Nothing," he dismissed. He accepted it a lot easier than Malaysia was doing at the moment.

～

MALAYSIA HAD STAKED OUT PABLO'S HOUSE UNTIL SHE spotted a familiar face. She had never met the woman but recognized Pablo's mother from the pictures he had of her in the house. The police had finished their work and stolen what they could before turning the house over to the family.

"Scuse me ma'am?" Malaysia said as she waddled up to the woman. Mrs. Hernandez looked classy in the pictures but even more so in person. Her son didn't need to be in the streets but chose that life, and got that death. Now she had to bury her baby boy. She reserved a plot next to his father on one side while the other was reserved for her.

"Yes?" She wondered and scrunched her face like people do when they look down on other people. She could see ghetto all over the pretty girl.

"I'm Malaysia," she informed but the name didn't seem to register with the woman.

"OK?" Mrs. Hernandez asked to see if more came with the name of a country she once visited.

"I'm, or I was, Pablo girlfriend," she said and placed her hand on the baby bump.

"And I assume you believe that child to be his?" She asked smugly, then cast a glance to little Trevor in the car seat. Whoever the girl was she was certainly pumping them out.

"Ion assume nothing! I know 'fo fact dis his baby!" She snapped in full ghetto girl splendor. Her hand went to a hip while her neck rolled as if on a swivel. Both seemed to amuse the sophisticated lady.

"Well, Pablo obviously can neither confirm or deny, so once the test are done..." Mrs. Hernandez said and trailed off since what else needed to be said until DNA could confirm or deny her claims.

"Until then, Pablo had our money in the, inside," she said and stopped just short of revealing where he stashed the cash. She didn't see the cops remove the safe so she assumed it was still safe.

"Again, my son is not here to confirm or deny. If there's money inside it is part of his estate," the snooty woman relayed but that went right over Malaysia's head.

"Look lady, we need our lil bread!" She snapped like she was ready to go there.

"Oh OK, I see," the woman suddenly agreed. "One moment please..."

"I know that's right!" Malaysia huffed to herself as Pablo's mother stepped aside to make a call. She mumbled something to someone before hanging up and turning back to Malaysia.

"One second please," she smiled pleasantly. Malaysia was stuck in ghetto girl mode since it seemed to work for her so far. Her face was still twisted up when the first of a few police cars arrived. Mrs. Hernandez's name rang bells and sent several cars responding to her 911 call,

"What seems to be the problem ma'am?" The first cop asked as he hopped out and placed a hand on his gun. He wouldn't let the fact that Malaysia was pregnant stop him from gunning her down if need be.

"A misunderstanding I'm sure?" Mrs. Hernandez asked Malaysia.

"Un-huh. A misunderstanding," she huffed and spun on her heels. More cars were pulling up as she pulled off but the woman told them she no longer felt threatened.

"Oh, I'll be back for that safe!" Malaysia vowed as the scene got smaller in her rear-view mirror. The scenery switched from chic to bleak when she arrived back to the city. Then from bad to worse as she drove hood to hood. She pulled to a stop in front of her grandmother's house and retrieved the baby from the car seat.

"Sup cuz!" Jose shouted and rushed the car. It was first come, first served any time Malaysia came over since she always broke bread. "Let me help with the baby!"

"Mmhm. Here!" She hummed and pushed a few ones his way.

"Thanks cuz!" He beamed even though it wasn't much.

"If you wanna make some real bread holla at me 'fo I go," she said and led the way inside.

"Lay-lay here!" One of the excited girls announced and she was soon mobbed. One of them relieved her of little Trevor and that was fine by her.

"Where granny at?" She asked peering between the kitchen and her bedroom.

"In here chile," she called from the kitchen. Malaysia walked in and joined her shucking peas. "What's wrong girl?"

"Trouble punk ass done kilt my man!" She whined and held Pablo's child in her stomach.

"That's a mouthful gal! Don't be saying that 'ifn you don't know fa 'sho!" She demanded. Granny knew Trouble was trouble in those streets but couldn't see that in him. She squinted to be sure, and still couldn't see it.

"Who else?" She asked but hushed on repeating the claim. It didn't matter since it was quietly being repeated in several hoods. Hoods with homeboys in the pen as well.

"News said it was a robbery. Trevor got plenty of money. Don't he?" Granny stated, then asked.

"Un-huh! Yeah!" Malaysia agreed even though it was no where near what he thought he had. If she could get the money from Pablo's she could put back what she took and still be up.

"Chile..." Granny warned and shook her head. It was all she needed to say about that.

"Look, I need a break. Can Trevor stay here with you? Just for a while?" Malaysia decided.

"That's exactly what yo mama said when she dropped you off here. She ain't made it back to get you yet," the wise woman warned. She would never turn any child away if a parent asked. Why leave a kid with a parent who doesn't want to parent it, was her motto.

"I ain't none of my mama!" She huffed with enough indignation to be believed.

"OK chile. Babies ain't cheap tho so dig in that expensive ass purse!" The woman said and stuck out her hand. Malaysia wanted to prove she was nothing like her mama and broke bread lovely. She parted with a mixed roll of money that lit the lady's eyes up. She didn't mind since she had a plan to make it all back.

"Still wanna make some bread cuz?" Malaysia asked Jose when she was leaving.

"Shit yeah!" He cheered just like she knew he would. The five grand payout she promised was enough to seal the deal. She gave him the address and particulars and went home to await his call.

~

"THIS IT?" PO-BOY ASKED NERVOUSLY FROM THE BACK SEAT. He was strictly a hood nigga and felt like a fish on dry land out here in these suburbs. All he saw were white people like it was the Grammy awards. The white people saw him too since they were riding in Doc's orange donk. If the car wasn't loud enough on its own the driver blasted the latest Doobie Daddie album. Heads turned the moment they turned into the well appointed subdivision.

"That's what the GPS say?" Doc asked and turned to Jose in the passenger seat.

"Hole up," said and made a quick call.

"You there?" Malaysia asked from the safety of her own apartment. She was smart enough to get her cousin and his friends to do the heavy lifting while she called shots from the sideline like a coach.

"Big ass house?" He asked as he looked up at it.

"White with black thangs on the windows?" She asked since she wasn't familiar with shutters.

"This is," he cheered ready to get to work. The five thousand they were splitting was nothing compared to what was in that safe but way more than they had ever seen. No one looked around to see the several parted mini blinds with eyes peering at them. By the time they reached the front door several 911 calls had already been placed.

"Step back and watch how a pro do it!" Doc said and pried the front door open. The trio had officially made the switch from trespassing to burglary.

"Just in case!" Po-boy said and whipped out a pistol. That added possession of a firearm in commission of a crime. Still they pressed on to add some more felonies.

"OK cuz, we in," Jose informed since Malaysia planned to walk them step by step. The police and Pablo's mom didn't stumble across the safe while searching so they wouldn't either. They wouldn't have to since Malaysia knew exactly where it was.

"OK look. Go into the first bedroom on the right," she directed and waited.

"Un-huh," Jose announced when he got there.

"In the closet. Lift up the carpet. From the corner," she spelled out.

"Ion see nothing?" He asked when her directions produced hard wood flooring beneath.

"You gotta lift the boards..." She said and waited for his reaction.

"Oh shit! It's safe under here!" He cheered. "What's the combination?"

"Yeah right!" She fussed and scrunched her whole face at the idea of letting him get in without her being present. She planned to pay them the five grand from her stash instead of even opening the safe in front of them. They would know just how bad they were getting chumped off if she did that. "Take the whole thang. I'll tell you where to meet me."

"OK cuz," José agreed as his two friends pried the steel safe out of the floor.

"Bruh, fuck that hoe! We can take this shit to the hood and open it!" Po-boy suggested.

"Bet you it's more than five damn racks in this bitch!" Doc agreed.

"Um, I can hear y'all niggas!" Malaysia snapped into her cousin's ear.

"Let me call you back!" Jose said and clicked off. "Fuck her!"

The trio was giggling real good as they carried the safe through the house. The laughter died in their throats when they opened the door to find half the police force posted up outside. They took position behind their cars in hopes of a shoot out.

"Hands in the air!" One cop shouted as the infrared beams danced on their torsos and faces. Doc let go of his end of the safe and raised his hands. Jose accepted defeat and raised his as well.

"I got this!" Po-Boy decided and went for his gun. The cops actually paused in disbelief as the moment they dreamed of manifested right before their eyes.

"Gun!" One cop screamed almost orgasmically. The quiet suburban block suddenly erupted in gun fire.

The poor boy managed to get a shot off but it slammed harmlessly into a car door. The police clapped back and lit them up. The race was on to pump as many rounds into their bodies before they hit the ground. All three died on their feet as the barrage of bullets held them up like puppets on strings. It was only the extra weight of all that lead that finally pulled them to the ground.

Malaysia and Trouble's chances of recovering the money were as dead as José, Po-Boy and Doc.

Chapter Twenty-Two

"*L*ook at you!" Shay cheered when she saw her sister in law for their weekly lunch date. Life can move real fast even in a slow town so they made sure to pump their brakes at least once a week to eat lunch.

"Cuz I'm happy!" Lalonda admitted almost defiantly. She had a tingle of regret in the back of her brain since technically she was committing adultery, but only because Malcolm was bucking on accepting service and signing the divorce papers.

She had them sent to Sheryl's house but she had the next man living with her already. He had been spotted here or there but she couldn't get a good address for him. She knew her brother knew something since he would get evasive and change the subject whenever she asked about him. It didn't matter since she had moved on. Her mind was settled and her heart was in New York.

"Well, like I said, you look happy!" Her sister in law repeated. They paused their conversation when the waitress came to the table and for good reason.

"How's my two favorite customers!" She greeted happily enough.

"Hey girl!" They sang back with phony smiles pasted on pretty faces.

"Girl, how about Judge Seeling was just here with his side piece!" She whispered and rambled on about everyone else's business.

"Um, excuse me, can we order, just real quick?" Lalonda snuck in when she had to take a breath.

"Mmhm, sure girl!" She said and took their orders and rushed off to fill it. They knew not to speak a word in front of the town gossip column.

"The check came the other day," Shay offered nonchalantly. It was a lot of money but didn't really make up for the years of her life spent in that awful place. "We ain't even put it in the bank yet."

"Knowing my brother, he finna keep on working," Lalonda laughed and shook her head. He was just like their father and had to do something. The elder Mr. Stanton had a good retirement check coming in but still worked at the new logging company to have something to do.

"He happy tho. We happy!" She said and laid her hand on their child moving around inside her.

"Mmph," Lalonda huffed and changed the subject. "I see he paid my bills again! I told y'all, I'm good!"

"Mmph," Shay retorted and changed the subject as well like they were playing Uno. "So, how's your lil friend?"

"He's not so lil, and he's good! Time is up and he's getting out!" She cheered.

"And then..." She asked excitedly. Shay envisioned them being like her and Chuck and living happily ever after.

"And then..." Lalonda repeated since she expected the same. Her and New York hadn't discussed anything further than the present. He said he loved her so what more needed to be said.

～

"COME ON BRUH. I GOT YOU A DETAIL WITH ME!" TROUBLE announced when his name was called that evening.

"What happened to the other guy?" Darius asked as he got dressed.

144

"New York goes home in the morning. This the best detail in the prison tho!" He assured him. That was debatable but at least there was no heavy lifting and no pots to scrub. "Plus ole chap being breaking us off with chicken biscuits!"

"Well, I do like those biscuits!" Darius admitted since Trouble usually passed off the extra New York gave him since he had Lalonda's mama's biscuits waiting on him. "What I gotta do?"

"Just do whatever she tell you and you can't go wrong," Trouble assured him. He could feel the eyes on him as he walked through the dorm. That was usual but today he felt a little extra heat. He turned and saw Lil-Zay wearing an evil snarl as he glared at him. He twisted his lips and kept pushing since he wasn't in the mood for his shit at the moment. Right now was time for Motown greatest hits chaplain Gayle style and chicken biscuits.

"Everything OK?" Darius asked when he felt that same heat exuding around the dorm.

"Hell yeah!" He shot back smugly. He was Trouble after all, and people moved when he said move. The rumors of him killing Pablo were spreading like Corona virus once did.

"Ion know 'bout dat shit shawty?" Lil-Bop said, shaking his head. He was in awe of Trouble and couldn't see him doing any slime shit like that.

"That's what the skreets is saying. Plus, if'n it was them bitch ass Rollers, then why he won't mash the button so we can smash on they ass?" Lil-Zay reasoned. His reasoning was tainted by rumors as well as the methamphetamine he snorted earlier.

"Gotta get all the facts shawty. We all eating off big bruh. He not finna fuck that up for nothing," Bop said hopefully. That's the thing about a lie. Enough people say it, it becomes a truth. Maybe not thee truth but still a truth. And that's enough to get someone killed.

"Here is our new man!" Trouble announced when Darius reached the chapel area. "Chaplain Gayle meet Darius. Darius, Chaplain Gayle."

"Pleasure to meet you ma'am," he offered with a nod.

Trouble took note of the etiquette and added it to the other lessons he was learning.

"Likewise. Have a seat so we can talk," she offered.

"I'll go get started," Trouble suggested and set off to get set up for church. Once again he set the chairs off from each other. It wasn't social distancing but so they couldn't reach each others dicks while she was putting on.

Trouble had never held a job on the streets but did enjoy working. Especially the satisfaction that comes from a completed job. He noticed he was done setting up chairs and Darius still hadn't joined him. He looked over to the office just as he staggered out. Darius's eyes looked heavy and he yawned like he was ready for a nap.

"Bruh, don't tell me you let her anoint you?" He asked trying not to laugh.

"But, you said, do whatever she said do?" He asked to make sure that's what he indeed told him.

"I meant empty the trash, mop the floor!" He cracked up. The situation was funny enough but the look on his face was priceless.

"Well, that oil was good and slick! I guess I kinda needed that," he admitted and cracked up with him. They saw the bulge in each pocket from the bottles of anointed oil she gave him to go and laughed even harder.

The night passed on like most and was inevitable for someone to get caught in a sex act. Still, more got away with it than get caught which made it worth their while. They earned their chicken biscuits for the night and headed back to the dorm.

"I don't got, have, any anointed oil so I'm finna stop and get my dick sucked," Trouble laughed some more as they made their way back to the dorm. He took a detour to the kitchen to see big Jessie. He was relieved not to see a line outside when he arrived. That meant no waiting so he walked up and knocked on the door.

"Come in!" A voice he didn't recognize called back from inside. He wore a curious face as he turned the knob and went inside.

"Where's Jessie?" He asked Bessie who was behind the desk.

"She ain't come in today. You must be Trouble? She always 'talmbout some dang trouble!" She giggled and shook the room. Jessie was around three and a quarter but Bessie was flirting with five hundred. Pussy by the pound indeed.

"Oh OK then," he sighed and turned to leave.

"Shit, you may as well get yo dick sucked while you here," she offered. It sounded quite reasonable so he did just that. It sure beat beating off with anointed oil.

Trouble was good and sleepy from the blow job when he returned to the dorm. Darius was already snoring by the time he came in. He still pulled his phone out and called big Jessie.

'The number you have reached has been changed to a non published number...'

"HERE YOU GO BRUH. THIS ALL YOU!" NEW YORK DECLARED as he packed his personal belongings. That consisted of his pics and letters. The rest he was leaving to his bunk-mate.

"All this?" The grateful man asked in disbelief. The food, books, free world socks and drawers weren't much but were also a lot for someone with nothing. The old timer lost all his family to time and now only got what the state gave him. That wasn't much so this was Christmas, Kwanzaa and Cinco de Mayo all wrapped up in one. "The house shoes too?"

"House shoes too dad," he laughed and gave him a hug. He wished he could take the man with him but it doesn't work like that.

"Ready to get to that woman of yours I bet!" He grinned and he was right.

"Hell yeah!" New York cheered and rubbed his hands together. He and Lalonda spent most of her shift inside the mop closet with him inside of her.

"New York, pack it up!" The officer announced when the call came for him to send him to intake for outtake.

"I'm already packed up!" He laughed. New York was met

with cheers as he made his way through the dorm. Good character while being here allowed for a good send off from people happy to see him going home.

"Good luck out there," the officer said as he let him out of the dorm one last time. New York didn't believe in luck but understood the sentiment and thanked him.

"If you're ever in New York..." He replied but left it there since there was nothing else to it. After the fluke charge that turned his Georgia visit into an extended stay in prison he just wanted out the whole state.

The air outside the gate seemed so much cleaner than the air inside. It was the same air, being free just made it seem fresher. He scanned the parking lot for familiar faces and found one.

"Hey!" Lalonda cheered and bounced by her car. She looked even better in a pair of tight jeans that showed off the Stanton sister's trademark fat asses. New York tilted his head curiously as he walked briskly to her. His head was still on a swivel as he continued to look around.

"Hey ma, what are you doing here?" He asked with his face scrunched. They talked about everything over the last few months but never this. Things had changed since then though.

"Well, surprise!" She cheered and handed him some flowers. Her uniforms were freshly washed and folded on the back seat ready to turn in. Right next to the clothes and shoes she bought for him. Her hand held a small picture she had made for him.

"Yeah but..." He was saying as another car pulled swiftly in since it was slightly late. Lalonda eyes followed his to the car as it pulled to a stop. The wheels had barely stopped rolling before the doors swung open. A cutie pie of a little girl was first out. Followed by a boy wearing his father's face. They raced over and leapt into his arms.

"Daddy!" The little girl squealed. She squealed even louder when he planted kisses all over her face. The boy wanted some attention too but was used to his little sister ruling the planet.

Lalonda couldn't help but to smile at the touching family

reunion. Her own disappointment had yet to register. It wasn't until a pretty lady with a yellow complexion got out and spread a bright smile. New York blinked and smiled when he saw her. The kids didn't complain when he turned from them and embraced their mother.

"Hey baby!" She purred and killed Lalonda's last delusion of her being his sister when his tongue slipped into her mouth. The girl giggled while the boy looked disgusted at his daddy kissing a girl.

Lalonda eased into her car while the family reunited. She could only hope no one who mattered saw the incident since she suddenly needed her job again. It got a little worse when she realized she still clutching the picture. She pouted and sat the ultrasound of their daughter on the front seat and pulled away. Her eyes burned from the tears but she managed to make it out of the parking lot.

Chapter Twenty-Three

"OK now Rallo! I cain't keep covering yo shorts!" Deputy Warden Davis said below.

"You want me, to, keep, licking this, pussy don't, you?" He asked as he licked. He may not have been much of a businessman but he did do a bang up with the box. She initially covered his short in exchange for some dick but now she was in love.

"Mmhm!" She hummed and bust a nut in his mouth. He clamped his lips over hers and took it all until she stopped shivering.

"Mmhm is right!" He laughed as he took position between her legs. He had to give her a hard time for checking him so he slapped her box with his hard dick a few times.

"Go on and put it in!" She squealed and took action. Nobody had time for his games so she reached out and pulled him inside of her. She grabbed his hips and worked her body against his.

"Just finna take the dick huh!" Rallo laughed. Playtime had come to an end when he pushed her large legs towards the ceiling and adjusted his footing. He got a good stance and commenced to beating the box like a bass drum.

Rallo was extra short this week for a couple reasons. One was he was now a whole meth addict who got high on his own supply. A supply fronted to him by the administration. Then, he was rewarded with some good, hot pussy for coming up short. A good portion of his money went to Reecie so some good could come out of it.

His young cousin kept him in tuned with what was going on in the streets as well as provided plenty pussy pics for him to share with his Rollers. Not to mention she was the perfect person to spread his narratives. Thanks to them, the lie about Trouble killing Pablo had taken legs. It now sounded so believable the actual shooters believed it.

"You, make me, damn, sick!" Davis grunted before she began to shiver and shook.

"I know!" He laughed and picked up the pace so he could get off before she tapped out. He gunned and hummed until he bust a nut of his own. "Shit! You got a bomb ass shot!"

"That's why I'm not covering for you no more! Get our bread right man!" She insisted as she pushed him out of her. Once again she made sure the rubber didn't bust inside of her. A sigh of relief escaped her lips since he was on borrowed time if he came up short again. Warden Mays would have had him wacked and replaced had she not intervened. The ball was in his court now.

"I'm good next week. Got me some more manpower!" He bragged since he couldn't hold water.

"I heard! What's up with that? The Muslims converted to Rollers?" She asked and twisted her face.

"Them niggas ain't sincere. They do the same shit we be doing!" He replied since no one respected the renegades.

"Hmmm," she hummed in thought. She knew Rabbit was leaving soon and so was Dino. Now she lost the so-called Muslims since the practicing ones wouldn't get with her program. She needed him to step up to make up for the slack. If not, she wouldn't intervene the next time her boss mentioned wacking his ass. Little did she know she was in jeopardy of losing the Riders since a mutiny was brewing within that camp as well.

"Let me go hit this yard," he said and fixed his clothes so he could look presentable when he left her office. Futile since he was going to brag to anyone who would listen that he just got laid.

∾

"YARD CALL!" THE OFFICER ANNOUNCED AND SET THE MEN IN motion. Technically she was supposed to sign each one out according to dorm and bed but that was too much work. The woman had a boyfriend she was eager to spend some time with so she popped all the doors and let the men do them. Everyone would be back by the next count so she wasn't worried about it.

Men used the security lapse to sneak into other dorms for various reasons. Some like her had boyfriends and wanted to get laid. Some went to get high, or join a poker game. Others used to time to get intricate artwork etched into their skin by one of the tattoo men. Then, of course their was the fuck shit. This is D-block and there's always some fuck shit going down.

"Watch yo self!" Jahil snapped when someone bumped into him in the hall extra hard. Hard enough to hurt and make him look down.

"Excuse, me. My, bad!" The man said and thrust his homemade knife with each word. He walked away as quickly as he had walked up and passed the knife off. A toothless smile spread on Shakur's weathered face when he kept his promise. "Told you I was gone get yo ass!"

"Fuck wrong with you?" Another Rollers asked when Jahil leaned against the wall. He had been right next to him but didn't see him get stuck.

"Some one, just, I got poked!" He grunted when he figured it out himself. It was far fewer wounds than he inflicted on Fuck-Shit but this was for that. That eye for that eye, wounds equal for equal.

"When? By who? Where?" his partner asked as he looked him over. The wounds weren't immediately visible until they all began to spring a leak.

"Ion know?" Jahil asked and looked around. Truth be told

he had done so much fuck shit it could have been anybody. "I need to go lay down!"

"Naw shawty, you need to take yo ass to medical!" he corrected and he was right. Jahil was ignorant enough to try to go sleep off the puncture wounds but he sank to the ground instead.

"Say officer! We need help!" the Roller shouted as he looked around for the dorm officer. He wasn't going to find her though because she was ducked off in a cell with the flap up, getting dug out. He summoned another Roller and they carried him off to medical themselves. Meanwhile, life moved on at yard call.

∾

"WHAT THE FUCK IS THIS GUY UP TO?" GHOST GRUMBLED AS Rabbit took more meetings without him. He was supposed to be next in line but was clearly being kept in the dark.

"Beats me?" The man shrugged since no one knew exactly what Rabbit was doing.

"First the spics, then the niggers. Now the spics again!" Ghost recalled since he was keeping tabs. He squinted at Rabbit and Fitz as they walked the track and tried to read their lips.

"Remember that old trailer park!" Rabbit began with a chuckle at the not so fond memory.

"Of course," Fitz nodded since it was his last place on earth before getting locked up Something they both shared.

"Well, I bought it," he added and waited for a reaction before continuing. He got it but it wasn't exactly the reaction he expected.

"I know. You bought it from me," the Mexican replied and finally laughed. He had began liquidating his assets as the years went on since he knew this charge carried deportation along with the prison time. He wouldn't fight it like some do. He had enough money to live like a king in Mexico.

"Hmp, OK. Well, I cleared it out. Put up a big ass triple wide. Got a brand new F-350 sitting out front," Rabbit said as if he could see it now. He saw it every day since he had pictures on his phone.

"You must have gotten some good news?" The savvy Mexican figured. People make moves like that once they can see the light at the end of this tunnel.

"Any day now. That's what I wanted to talk with you about," he acknowledged. His own people didn't know Rabbit had been granted parole.

"You want to sell your mule," Fitz said knowingly. A good mule is far too valuable to just give away, that's why he made plans.

"Not sell, give. You can have the mule and the connect. All I want is a cut. Twenty percent," he offered. He knew the Mexicans had product and a mule but the product was trash so they only got the scraps. Fitz turned to face him and ponder the proposal. His head shook once, before beginning to nod.

"We have a deal!" Agreed. They shook on it making Ghost even more suspicious.

"Looks like they made some kind of deal?" JC guessed.

"Yeah. And I think I know what?" Ghost growled. "He's fucking playing us! It's time to get him out of the picture! We're going to kill him tonight!"

"Rabbit season!" He agreed since he would move up to the number two spot. The perfect spot to plot his own coup one day.

～

"BRUH, YOU GOT SOMETHING ON YOUR MIND?" TROUBLE finally asked. He had been ignoring Lil-Zay's glaring at him since they came out. He was already in a foul mood after Pablo and then came the news his younger cousin José got killed by the cops. To top all that off now he couldn't reach Jessie.

"Cuz, niggas saying you had something to do with bruh getting kilt," he revealed out loud what was being whispered about.

"Jose? My family? Who the fuck said that shit? Say it to my face!" Trouble exploded. The outburst drew attention from all in earshot.

"Nah, Pablo. Cuz he was smashing your baby mama," Lil-Bop put out because he needed to know. Trouble was his hero but that's some real live fuck shit if he did it.

"Listen," Trouble said loud and slow to make sure everyone heard every word. "Yeah, bruh was smashing baby mama. Facts, but I'm the one who put him on the broad. Pablo was my 'muhfuckin potna! We was getting bread together! The fuck I'ma kill the nigga for and fuck up my bread?"

Trouble paced the bleachers to look in every face. Whoever didn't believe him could speak up now or forever hold their tongue. Every face dipped or ducked in his presence, except one.

"Who else then? And why you won't let us ride on them fuck ass Rollers?" Zay demanded.

"Cuz I said so! Cuz I run this shit! That's the fuck why!" Trouble said so close to his face his lips touched his nose while he spoke. Lil-Zay just pouted, huffed and puffed but kept his mouth shut. The appearance of a helicopter above brought officers out to clear the yard.

"Yard over! Back to the dorms!" They instructed as the helicopter began to descend. It stopped and hovered as they communicated with the medical staff, then pulled up, up and away. "Never mind..."

"Someone ain't make it?" Rallo laughed when the helicopter began to disappear from sight. Little did he know it was one of his who just passed.

"Uh-oh," Shakur said to himself when the helicopter left. He was the one who caused it by sticking Jahil in the hall. He was also smart enough to move in silence and even his own brothers around him had no idea what he just did. His shoulders shrugged since it was what it is and he was cool with it.

Chapter Twenty-Four

"*I* know, I know," Shay moaned as she sought to console her inconsolable sister in law. The woman heaved big sobs and big tears while blowing snot bubbles from her nose. An ugly cry to the highest degree.

"I feel so stupid!" Lalonda moaned and wiped her face. The nosey waitress kept trying to steal a glimpse but scowls from Shay kept her at bay.

"It's not your fault. He was dead wrong for leading you on! Ugh! These dudes gas chicks up to do a bid with them knowing they going back to they baby mama when they get out!" Shay fussed like she had some expertise on the matter.

"Well..." Lalonda admitted since technically he never promised her anything. It was she who assumed they would continue their love affair when he got out. He told her he loved her and she had no reason to doubt him. He did, he just loved his wife and children more.

"Girl don't tell me you never asked what his plans were? Tell me y'all did talk about all this!" Her sister in law demanded.

"We just lived in the moment," Lalonda said and accepted it for herself at that moment. There would be no more tears from then on so she used her shirt to clear off the residue.

SA'ID SALAAM

"Well the moment is over. And you still..." Shay was saying but the look on Lalonda's face said there was more. "What?"

"Girl..." She twisting her lips, shook her head and passed her the ultrasound picture.

"Nuh-uh! No you ain't bitch!" She said and refused to accept it. That got a well needed laugh out of Lalonda.

"Chile, we was screwing every dang night. Ain't never use nare rubber," she admitted. There would be no more head shakes either since she accepted that as well.

"Ooooh! I'm, I'm, I'm telling Chuck!" Shay whined and pulled her phone.

"Girl I'm the big sister. He cain't do nothing to me!" Lalonda laughed but Shay kept calling. She wasn't calling to snitch but to warn.

"What you calling me for? You know we were on the way!" Chuck asked as they arrived. They as in him and Malcolm. "Made me think your water broke!"

"Come on!" She said and pulled him away by force. She filled him in as they left Lalonda and her husband behind. His eyes went wide and he ended up pulling her.

"Hey," Malcolm offered contritely. He knew the woman before him well enough to know she just had a good cry and assumed it was over him. "Can I sit?"

"You can," she shrugged nonchalantly, then quickly covered the ultrasound picture with her hand. "What Malcolm? You finally signed the papers?"

"Nope. Not going to," he offered plainly. "That's giving up. I'm not giving up on us."

"Ain't no us! You saw to that! Made sure of that!" She shot back to the waitresses satisfaction.

"Yeah, I did. I lost my dang job and lost myself. Started to pity myself and started dranking. I knew I didn't deserve a woman like you so I..." He was saying but couldn't manage to get that part out. Lalonda knew she still loved him when the pain in his eyes made her heart ache as well. All she ever wanted was what they had but he took that away.

"Mmhm," she hummed so he went on.

"I'm back me tho! I'm Malcolm again! I done stopped

158

dranking and go to them classes. I been working with yo daddy and Chuck for months," he informed.

"Hmp!" She huffed now that she understood why Chuck acted funny anytime she asked about him. "So, you the one been paying my bills?"

"Yup. While renting a room or sleeping in the truck. As long as you good I'll sleep in the woods!" He declared. She couldn't doubt him though because the Malcolm she married would do anything for his woman.

"It's too late now Malcolm," she said fought not to cry again. He was the only man she ever wanted and he was back, but she was gone.

"Ain't never too late! Love don't got no limit! Love ain't got a clock!" He said and smiled since it sounded fly.

"I um, I, I was seeing somebody," she admitted in a whisper that pissed the waitress off since she missed it.

"I don't care! You know about ole gal so, I, I um, yeah, Ion care!" He accepted. He did care but he did it so he had to accept it.

"There's more to it," she said and pulled her hand away to uncover the ultrasound. Malcolm tilted his head curiously at the picture. He knew exactly what it was but it took a few moments to apply it to their conversation.

"Chuck and Shay?" He asked hopefully. The same hope people allow themselves when filling out a lottery ticket. Knowing good and damn well what the answer is. He did too so Lalonda didn't need to say a word. Malcolm quietly contemplated for a moment before his mind was made up. He let out a sigh and scooted his chair back to stand. He cracked a parting smile to wish her well and turned to leave.

"Knew you was a coward," she said to his back as he departed. The sharp words stopped him in his tracks. He felt all the eyes from Chuck and Shay sitting in their car, to the nosey waitress spying nearby. They all saw the slow smile form on his face as he turned again.

"You still seeing him?" He asked but her head was shaking before he got the question all the way out. "You ready to leave that damn job?"

"Yes," she pouted submissively.

"Come on then. Let's go home!" Malcolm said and extended his hand. Manning up it always easy, but its always best. Malcolm had to live with all the results of his actions. Even if it meant raising the next man's kid.

～

"ARGGH!" GHOST GRUNTED AFTER SNORTING A LONG LINE OF meth up both nostrils. It was the fuel to gas him up to do what needed to be done. He had to be the one to do it too or people could question his rule. "To be the king, you have to kill the king."

Word spread easily through the disgruntled ranks of the White Boys and every one agreed to pledge allegiance to Ghost once the deed was done. It helped that he promised more dope since Rabbit had slowly began cutting everyone out. The last drop went straight to the Mexicans. Now they were becoming buyers instead of sellers.

The White boys in the dorm nodded at Ghost when he made his move to murder the king. Waiting until last count is always best so the body won't get discovered until the next day. Depending on who was working that is because some officers wouldn't even notice a dead body.

"To be the king..." Ghost said to himself at Rabbit's door. He took a few breaths to hype himself up and eased inside. Rabbit was sleeping on his back under the blanket which made it easy for a coward.

Merle was technically assigned to the bottom bunk but Rabbit had commandeered it when he moved in. The older man was bundled up under his blankets on the top bunk when he came in.

"White power!" He grunted and shoved the knife into the sleeping man's throat. He pressed his body weight until he felt the tip of the blade touch his spine. A rush of warm blood gushed out and soaked the blanket. Ghost smiled broadly as he turned and walked out of the cell.

"Hail Ghost! White power!" The White boys hooped and

hollered at the hanging of the guard. Rabbit had served them well but he was gone now. Rabbit season had come to a close with a dead rabbit.

∼

"STAND FOR COUNT," THE MORNING SHIFT OFFICER BARKED and banged on the door frame of Rabbit's cell. Some officers let the inmates sleep and would just count them in their rack. Jolly was not one of those officers. It may take him longer to get everyone up and standing but he didn't mind. If he couldn't sleep they wouldn't sleep. He got no reply the second time he banged so he barged in and snatched the top blanket away.

"Huh?" He wondered of the clothes and blankets rolled underneath. That's when he noticed the dried pool of blood on the bottom blanket. He pulled it away and saw old Merle looking up at dead people stuff. He backed out calling it in and shouting to the inmates, "Lock down! Lock it down!"

The dead people code didn't garner much haste since they would still be dead whenever they arrived. Curious faces filled most of the windows in the doors as nosey niggas wanted to see what happened so they could spread the news. None of the White boys watched since they already knew.

"What we got?" Sergeant Quick asked as he came into the dorm.

"Got on deceased on the bottom. Top bunk is empty!" He reported.

"Let see your roster," The CERT sergeant took the roster to verify the names.

"In the booth," the old man said since he usually used a cheat sheet to count, then notate the roster accordingly.

"Good help really is hard to find isn't it?" The Sarge asked the other CERT officer as the old man ran in slow motion to retrieve the clipboard containing the roster. Jolly decided he would walk back so he had time to fill in what should have been done upon arrival. His head tilted when he saw the cell only contained one person.

"Looks like that's Merle Swan," he said confirming he was in that bed.

"And the empty rack?" The CERT officer asked turning sideways to look at the corpse.

"Johnson, Robert. Looks like he signed protective custody last night?" Jolly realized. Ghost and the rest would get the news later. They killed the wrong man because Rabbit skipped out on them before they could get to him. He wasn't the only one seeking solace in solitary confinement prior to release. Some prisons will lock an inmate down for up to a week prior to release. Some inmates will lock themselves down for even longer when they get short.

～

"SAY ORDERLY, GET ME A LIGHT?" RABBIT ASKED WHEN THE breakfast trays were picked up. He had made sure to bring enough tobacco, weed and books to last the week he had left.

"A dollar," the orderly said and came over with a lighter. Rabbit pushed a honey bun under the door in exchange for the light. He wisely lit a wick so he wouldn't have to keep paying him all day.

"Appreciate it," he said and took a deep drag that he almost choked on when he heard his name called. It wasn't his name that shocked him, just who was calling it.

"Rabbit! That you?" Dino called out from the next cell. The anxiety of his pending release caused him to seek refuge here as well. All he had known was prison and confinement. The prospect of freedom literally scared him to death. He flirted with the idea of killing someone so he could stay. Instead he chose life and locked himself down.

"Not One Eyed Dino in PC?" Rabbit reeled. Usually only the weak caught protective custody.

"Yup, right next to you!" Dino reminded and laughed. "They uh, they said I can..."

"Hard to even say ain't it!" Rabbit laughed. He knew the feeling since he had yet to say the words out loud himself. Not even to himself.

"Lets say it together? Same time!" Dino suggested and counted it down. "Three, two, one..."

"I'm going home!" They both announced and giggled wildly at the idea of it. They had different release dates the next week but it was finally over.

"So, what you gonna do out there?" Rabbit asked without a trace of the hatred he once harbored towards the man. At one point he couldn't get a good bowel movement without being reminded of the abuse he suffered at his hands. Well, it wasn't his hands but...

"Um, Ion know?" He admitted since it was hard to think that far. "Thanks to you and my hustle, I'm way up."

"You're welcome," Rabbit shot back. They both were way up from hustling behind the wall.

Most inmates were only going home with the thirty five dollar debit card the state handed out. It didn't matter if someone did a hundred years, all they were getting was the thirty five bucks. Unless they had money on their books to go with it. Both Dino and Rabbit kept a few thousand dollars on their books for this occasion, but both also had plenty of money put away. They knew this day could one day come and well prepared for it.

"Well, I got me a nice piece of land. Brand new house and truck. Finna go live until I die," Rabbit announced proudly.

"I want some pussy," Dino admitted and pouted in his cell. Rabbit could relate since he had never had a woman either. Once again the prospect of freedom consumed them both and muted the conversation. They would speak more before they departed. It just wouldn't be now.

Fitz was a couple cells down waiting on immigration to come pick him up. They planned to kick him out of the country and ban him from ever returning. The man had a few million dollars as well as a four thousand acre ranch paid for by the drug addicts of America, so he didn't need to come back. In the meantime he just sat, and listened.

Chapter Twenty-Five

"*F*ucking fucked us!" Ghost moaned when the White boys convened on the yard. Merle molested too many people in his own family for them to give a fuck about him. That meant they could write his murder up as a suicide and take him 'out back'.

"That fucking guy..."JC said, shaking his head. He would never admit it out loud but he liked how the man moved. Selling the connect to the Mexicans was a shrewd business move that kept his share in tact. Ghost planned on fucking him out of that share but Rabbit fucked him first. He who fucks first fucks best, or whatever.

"So, what now we're supposed suck Mexican dick for meth?" He fussed. He meant it rhetorically but that's exactly what would eventually happen with some of the junkies in their ranks. All that was left was what was still in rotation. Rabbit wasn't getting paid on that so he searched for a way to flip it. At the same time a way was looking down at him.

"I don't know?" Warden Mays said skeptically as she watched the White boys minus their leader Rabbit.

"A bunch of fucking junkies!" Davis huffed. Her snitches kept her in the loop with most of what was going on around the compound.

"So is that Rallo guy you're fucking," her boss reminded,

then laughed at the reply written on her face. "There's not much that goes on around here that I don't hear about!"

"I know that's right!" Davis laughed in relief since she must not have heard about her pussy by the pound operations or she would have wanted in.

She couldn't help but admire the woman's hustle game. The warden recently caught wind of much the man who ran the gambling tickets made and taxed him too. All the 'store men' charging 'one for two' back and cashing out PayPal, cash app and green dots had to chip in as well.

"Well, we lost our Muslim connect. The White boys as well as the Bandos. What's next?" The warden sighed.

"Looks like trouble with the Riders," Davis guessed as she watched Trouble walk the track alone while Lil-Zay addressed the gang. Mays turned to watch how this would unfold.

"FIRST, HE BEEFING WITH BRUH 'BOUT THE BITCH! THREE, HE ain't tryna clap back!" Zay said as he made his case to the rest of the Riders. Only a few caught that he didn't know his numbers very well, but he was making sense. Most of them were just as high as he was so it sounded good.

"I feel you bruh, but bruh got the connect," Lil-Bop reminded. He was one of the few sober ones but his loyalty was to his pocket. He had love for Trouble but didn't care who ran the show as long as he was eating.

"Shit, we got the connect! We the ones moving the shit! He just eating off our hustle!" Lil-Zay fumed. He made it sound bad even though that's how it's supposed to be. Yeah they were the ones grinding but there wouldn't be shit to grind without a connect. Without a boss.

"Or we can get it like the Rollers be getting it!" One who longed for the lawlessness of the Rollers cheered. Trouble held them back from the bullshit and urged them to get their GEDs and stack their money. That appealed to some but most were street niggas to death and wanted no parts on anything positive.

"Hell yeah!" Another cosigned and the revolution was official.

"Tell bruh he need to come holla at us!" Zay barked and puffed his chest. The meth had him feeling like Superman so he was ready to leap a tall building in a single bound. A young one looking for points rushed off to carry out the mission.

"Fuck!" Trouble groaned when he saw the kid rushing towards him. He had seen the animated speech Lil-Zay was giving in his absence and knew nothing good was coming his way.

"Aye shawty, Lil-Zay say you need to come holla at him!" He barked with the same energy he was sent with. That was half the battle, the other half was to keep that same energy.

"Or what!" Trouble barked back and made the kid cower in fear. He could have mashed the gas on the guy but that would defeat the very conclusion he had come to while walking in circles. "A'ight. Here I come..."

"We finna smash bruh if he don't step off," Zay said for support.

"Naw shawty, 'ifn you finna get the whip you gotta shoot a one with him," one Rider acquainted with the rules informed. The rest agreed as Trouble arrived, literally and figuratively.

"You, sent for, me?" Trouble asked with inflection on 'you' as in who is you, and 'me' as in to send for me. It had always been Trouble who sent for people and people came running.

"Yeah my nigga," Lil-Zay nodded and bobbed as he hyped himself up. He knew he couldn't beat Trouble head up but the meth coursing through his system said 'maybe'. Then the devil whispered in his ear and cosigned, 'you the man'. That's what the devil does but it not his ass or him going to jail.

"Well, here I am!" He snapped and checked the surrounding faces. They were split so this would have to play itself out.

"Nigga, we don't like the way you handling the whip! You need to step off or we can shoot the one," Zay demanded.

"Let's hit then!" Trouble agreed and took a fighters stance. He had already made up his mind to leave the gang but going out without a fight would be pussy. Trouble was no pussy.

"Argh!" Lil-Zay grunted and threw a few wild hay-makers that hit nothing but air. Had he been fighting the air it may have been a knock out. He wasn't though and Trouble side-steps the punches and popped him with a two piece.

Trouble passed on the uppercut that would have ended both the fight and the coup. He saw the fear in Zay's eyes like a person who jumped in the wrong side of a pool. Looking for shallow water and realizing they're in over their head.

Trouble threw an uncharacteristic wild punch which Zay slipped just like Trouble had taught him. Trouble knew what should follow since he taught that too. He clenched his body for the body shots he knew where coming.

'This shit actually works!' Lil-Zay thought to himself as he dipped the punch and countered with two body shots, followed by a hook.

"Ooooh!" The yard exclaimed when Trouble went down. Rallo watched with glee since he was a hater but also confused at how easily the smaller man whooped him.

Trouble could have easily been the one standing over the over one instead of the one being stood over. He knew if he won this fight he would still be stuck as the head of the Riders. This was his way out so he took it.

"Stay down my nigga!" Zay demanded and hoped he would.

"You got that. We good," Trouble managed while managing not to choke on his pride.

"I got the whip now! Anyone got a problem with that?" Lil-Zay dared like a big man. He looked in every face to be sure. Every head shook and the crown had been passed. He extended his hand to his fallen foe to show respect. Trouble took it and stood. "Y'all still show this man some respect! Bet not nare nigga fuck with him!"

Trouble managed to hold his smile until he reached the dorm and made it to his cell. Darius was already inside pacing the small space. He had seen the fight on the yard and wondered what was to come.

"Sup," Trouble greeted way happier than he should be for

someone who just got whooped and kicked out the gang. Darius had no idea he controlled the fight and the outcome.

"Man are you OK?" He said while looking for bumps or bruises and finding none. Most times when the gangs got on someone they missed a week of commissary since they couldn't log on to the kiosk.

"I'm better than OK!" He said since he was. He was finally free.

Chapter Twenty-Six

"*J*ohnson, let's ride!" The officer said with a wide smile. Some officers were just hateful and hated to see anyone go home. He was not one of them and was excited to see someone get a second chance at life.

"Let's ride!" Rabbit cheered and smiled his one toothed smile.

"What's the first thing you finna do?" One eye Dino asked again as Rabbit collected the few papers going with him. They had talked about it every day they had spent in segregation but it never got old.

"Gonna get me some pussy!" He said and shook his head as he could taste it already. The one thing the two enemies had in common was neither had ever had a woman. That's why it was at the tip top of each list.

"How you gone hit it!" Dino cheered.

"Like this, this, this! Un, un, un!" Rabbit grunted as he demonstrated his stroke. It probably wouldn't please a woman but he didn't know any better. "A nice big titty blonde! You're up next bruh!"

"Two more days!" Dino said as they came eye to eyes at his cell. They once wanted to kill each other but now they just gave a parting nod. Rabbit next stopped in front of Fitz's cell since immigration hadn't come yet. He would be leaving soon as well, but straight to a flight to Mexico.

"Mi amigo," Rabbit nodded. They had exchanged info since they still had business together.

"Mi amigo," Fitz replied with a faint smile.

"You staying or..." The officer asked and held the door that led to the hall. That hall led to the intake/outtake which led to freedom.

"Duh!" Rabbit laughed and quickly caught up with him. Dino was ready for a woman but still looked at his ass one last time before he left.

"No one is coming to get you?" The outtake officer asked rhetorically since he had a bus ticket. The eight thousand dollars on his check said he could get a ride better than Greyhound.

"Nah, I wanna look out the window without shackles," he admitted. The Georgia country side was lovely but he could never really enjoy it with hardened steel digging into his wrist and ankles.

"I can dig it," the cop said but he really couldn't. No one can until they spend hours on a bus or van getting bit by shackles. He finished transitioning the inmate back into a whole man and nodded his goodbye.

The transport officer was waiting as he came outside. Rabbit was disappointed when he saw the van but this time there were no cuffs, no shackles. He ignored the prison as they pulled away since he would never see the inside of one again. He would die free before living in imprisonment ever again.

"Good timing," the officer remarked as they arrived at the bus terminal.

"Huh?" Rabbit asked since his mind was moving to fast to see and hear.

"Never mind," he said since it wasn't relevant. He opened the door and watched Rabbit board the bus. Technically he was supposed to stay put until it pulled away but he pulled away instead. He should have just enough time to shoot home for a quick quickie on the clock. It would be like getting paid to get laid and ain't nothing wrong with that.

Rabbit settled in a middle seat with the excitement of a school field trip. Instead of the museum or zoo he was going to his own land and home. He leaned his head against the window and stared out the window as the bus traveled to his home town.

People boarded and got off at several steps along the way. He watched most with a distant curiosity until he saw her. The big titty blonde with the bright smile. The sun beamed through the sundress she wore and revealed she wasn't wearing panties. She scanned the bus like looking for someone to ride next to who wouldn't be creepy. Rabbit looked up at her in awe as she chose him.

"Hello," the blonde said with a warm smile on her thin lips. Rabbit was too busy inhaling the smell of a woman to speak. This was the closest he had been to a woman in over two decades.

"I'm sorry," he said when she shrugged his rudeness away. "I'm Rab, Robert."

"Rab-Robert?" She asked. She had heard odder names but wanted to get it right.

"Just Robert," he corrected and regained some composure.

"Christina," she said and extended her dainty hand to shake. Rabbit took a second to look and recall the last time he touched a woman. He couldn't and got an instant erection the second his hand touched hers. "Are you OK? You look light headed."

"Yeah, I um," he said and paused before telling too much of his business. "No. Your the first woman I've touched in twenty years! I just got out of David Blocker prison a couple hours ago."

"Twenty years! Omg! That's a long time!" She said like she was fascinated. Her smile spread as a wicked thought crossed her mind. "Come on!"

Rabbit wasn't sure what she had in mind when she led him to the pissy bathroom. They squeezed inside where she immediately shoved her tongue into his mouth. She reached down and freed the raging erection from the state issue release pants.

"Fuck!" He grunted when he felt her grip his dick and tug on it. It got even better when she dipped low and took him inside of her mouth. "Fuck, the fuck-fuck!"

She came up giggling and pushed him down on the seat. She quickly mounted him and rubbed the first real, live pussy on his dick. It felt nothing like the fee-fees dude swear feel like real pussy. The only thing that feels like real pussy is real pussy.

"Ssss," she hissed as she sank slowly down his dick. It didn't take long since he didn't have much dick.

"I um," Rabbit offered apologetically but didn't last long enough to finished. She hopped up just in time to see him skeet all over himself.

"Shhhhh!" Christina hushed and put her finger on his lips. His head tilted curiously when she took the call in rapid fire Spanish. That was odd but not as odd as when she passed him the phone.

"Me?" He asked but took the phone and put it to his ear.

"Mi amigo," Fitz said with a smile. Rabbit recognized the danger as soon as he recognized the voice. He then felt the burn of the straight razor she ran from ear to ear. Rabbit was too busy with the gush of blood escaping the gaping wound to prevent her from escaping. She snapped a picture before rushing from the pissy stall and left the occupied sign up.

Christina got off at Rabbit's stop and into a waiting car. It wasn't the only car waiting since Ghost had sent a ride as well. Rabbit betrayed the White boys and he sent some white boys to wack him. They only glanced over the big titty blonde Latina when she got off and kept watch on the door.

"The fuck?" One asked the other when everyone was off and no sign of Rabbit. He just shrugged since his guess was as good as his.

"Maybe he seen us?" The passenger suggested and got out. He tucked the pistol he planned to murder Rabbit with into his waistband and ran into the bus.

He pulled the gun and boarded the empty bus. He slowly crept along and pointed the gun between every seat as he made his way to the back. He scratched his head with the barrel of the gun when he reached the back seat and no sign of Rabbit. He wouldn't have thought to check the toilet but he did have to pee.

"Shole nuff!" He laughed when he found wide eyed Rabbit staring off into the after life. He didn't know what or who happened to him but decided to still take credit. He snapped a pic for proof and sent it to Ghost. He still had to pee so he pissed on Rabbit and shook his dick when he was done. "White power!"

Chapter Twenty-Seven

"$\mathcal{W}$ow! I mean just..." Dino said and searched his vast vocabulary for an appropriate word. He may have been a booty bandit but he was quite articulate. Yet all he could manage was another, "Wow!"

"Never even made it off the bus!" Nutty bar reported through the bars. He looked both ways before pulling a phone and showing him the picture of Rabbit seated on the toilet dead.

"He was double and triple crossing so many mufuckas, I wonder which one got his ass?" He said and shook his head.

"Fitz, your ride is here!" The officer announced as he came back to the floor.

"I am ready," Fitz said and stepped from the cell. He looked Dino in his eye and gave a nod as he left the building. Immigration was waiting outside to escort him from the country and that was the end of his story.

"Stick it through the flap one time," Nutty bar urged and licked his lips.

"What?" Dino reeled even though he was looking down at what he meant.

"Yo dick. One for the road!" The sissy whined. He was feeling unloved since Dino hadn't touched him in the weeks since he got the good news.

"Bruh chill! I ain't with that homo shit!" Dino snapped.

"Huh? Say what?" Nutty bar grimaced as he processed what was going on. "Oh, you brand new cuz you finna go home? Nigga you gay too!"

"Nah shawty! I ain't never sucked a dick or got hit in my ass!" He laughed. The joke was on him though because pitching is just as gay as catching. Nutty bar's face contorted in sorrow and he rushed off in tears.

Dino felt good about himself and sat back down to read some fiction. Something he rarely did his entire bid but now it helped pass the time in solitary. The urban fiction books gave him a distorted view of the life waiting for him outside these walls. He never thought he would make it back out again but soon heard his name called.

"Williams, let's ride," the officer called as he opened the cell. Dino stepped forward empty handed and prompted the question, "You don't have anything?"

"Nah," he said and shook his head. Most inmates will leave with letters and pics from their loved ones. Or at least a bible and some literature. He had nothing or no one so his hands were empty. They made the walk over to the outtake area in silence.

Dino had done so much fuck shit behind these walls he expected someone to come running saying, wait, it's a mistake. He can't leave here, but no one did. Like Rabbit he had a few thousand dollars on his books as well. Some went on the debit card while the rest went on a check. He had long ago hired a lawyer to help hold his money so he would have no trouble cashing it. It also allowed him to keep his money since he didn't have any love ones to steal from him.

"Bus ticket," the officer said and handed him a ticket to Atlanta. Dino just nodded since speech required breath and he had barely taken one since leaving the cell. The rest was a blur until he heard the transport officer speak up.

"Here we are. Make sure you get on that bus!" He warned since he wasn't sticking around. He had already called home and his wife was getting hot and gushy for him.

"Fa sho," he agreed and stepped out. He only took a step before his worst fear was realized.

"Wait!" The officer called and stopped him in his tracks. Dino slowly turned to face him before he spoke. "Be careful out there. The last one ain't even make it home!"

"I will," he assured him. Dino knew he had wronged as many people as Rabbit had if not more. It was his bullshit that created Rabbit in the first place. What's done can never be undone so he lifted his eye and boarded the bus.

If ever One eyed Dino longed for two eyes it was now. There were so many sights whipping by the window he wished he had three more eyes to take it all in. The sights got even better when he reached the bus station in downtown Atlanta. He stared across the street at the famous strip club Atlanta was famous for. He had heard many stories about getting head and a table dance fresh off the prison bus. Even free drinks for the newly free.

It may or may not have been true but Dino wouldn't find out. Not today since he had other business to attend to. He was very deliberate so he walked the few blocks over to his lawyers office. He got a good scare when he heard a sound he heard every day in the chain gang. He was so used to the Muslim call to prayer he could probably do it himself even if he didn't understand the words. He figured out why when he saw Muslim men, women and children filing into a masjid to answer that call. His regular breathing resumed and he continued on to his lawyers office.

"Dino Williams to see Mr Brown," he told the secretary.

"Yes sir. One second sir," the pretty white girl smiled and batted her eyes. She was a big titty blonde just like he and Rabbit had talked about. Dino tilted his head curiously at her behavior since he had no idea he had the looks the ladies liked. Girls still were saying his dark skin and thick liPS were ugly when he left the streets. Even the eye patch gave his rugged good looks a boost.

"Dino!" Mr Brown cheered and threw his arms wide when he saw his client. The ten percent of what he managed for the former inmate bought him the Porsche outside.

"Mr Brown," he nodded and accepted the hug. He expected it to come with the bad news that his money was gone. Over his twenty years he had seen plenty men hustling real good in the joint only to have someone they trusted fuck their money up.

"Come! Sit!" He said instead and pulled him into his office. Once they were comfortably seated across the desk from each other he began sliding items across to him, explaining each one as he went along. "You can check your balance against your own records. I've included deductions to pay taxes since you don't want that smoke."

"OK," Dino blinked at the million left. Twenty years of selling drugs, scams and fake tax schemes had paid off. He collected the rest of his paperwork and finally two sets of keys. "My place?"

"Yes. I'll have Tonya drive you!" The lawyer said excitedly. They stood and shook hands before he summoned his secretary to drive him over to the condo. She knew exactly where it was since she helped in the purchase of the place.

"My pleasure!" The woman gushed and bounced. Mr Brown knew then Dino was about to get some pussy even if he hadn't figured it out yet. It wasn't part of the service but he saw they way she looked at he added up to a we.

"If you need anything else..." Mr Brown offered along with his hand.

"I'll be sure to hit you up," Dino assured and shook his hand.

"Right this way!" Tonya sang and led the way to the elevator. She assumed her ass had an audience so she made sure to give him something to look at. Dino did look and realized he didn't need Nutty bar to prime him up anymore. He had a nice stiff erection by the time they reached the elevator.

Dino watched for her reaction when she stole the inevitable crotch glance. He had noticed the majority of women did since he came of age to notice such things. Tonya's eyes went wide when they just happened to run across the lump in his prison issue pants.

"We need to get you some new clothes!" She said an excuse when she looked up to see him looking down at her.

"Yes. I can't wait to get out of these clothes," he said and moistened her lace panties. He watched her ass wiggle as she led the way to her Audi. Dino liked the coupe but it was too small for him. He wasn't sure what he wanted to drive just yet but could afford whatever it was.

A few turns later they pulled into the underground parking of a downtown high rise. He followed the wiggling ass to another elevator and up to his floor. Dino had picked the condo himself online but seeing it in person made his dick even harder.

"Wow, this is great!" He said as they walked into the furnished unit. He had picked the furnishings as well and they complimented the view outside the floor to ceiling windows just perfectly. He wondered off in one direction to look around while she headed in another since she had been here before. Dino admired his well appointed and updated kitchen. The view from the balcony, bathroom, and finally the unit's one bedroom. The sights in there stole his whole vocabulary.

"Wow?" Tonya laughed since Dino seemed to be at a loss for words. Understandably since she was stretched out naked on his bed. She did part her pretty pussy with her fingers displaying the pink goodness inside.

"That's the word I was looking for," he laughed and gave her something to wow about when he stripped out of his clothes and showed what twenty plus years of push ups and pull ups can do. Plus the dick. She crawled forward to meet him as he approached and opened her mouth. "Un-uh!"

"No?" She asked since no one ever turned her down for head before. Dino had gotten plenty of head in his life, albeit from men, but still, had never touched a real vagina.

"No. Let me," he explained and laid her back. He kissed from her tiny pink toes until he felt the heat from her vagina on his face. He admired it from close up before giving it a kiss. The kiss made her back arch of the bed and a hiss escape her lips. This would be the first time he ate some pussy but they are pretty self explanatory. He followed her gasp, hisses and moans until she came in his mouth.

"Fuck me! Fuck me!" She demanded and pulled him up face to face.

"I, um OK, how..." He was saying until she grabbed his dick and put it inside of her. "Oh my!"

"Oh my is right!" Tonya laughed since she knew what he was just finding out. She knew she had some good pussy but she had no idea it was his first. She also had no idea this handsome specimen of black manhood had been fucking men for the last two decades. Lucky for her he somehow managed to evade the deadly virus in circulation throughout the prison system. It was why most of the 'gay for the stay' dudes came home and infected wives, baby mamas and girlfriends. Niggas really need to pick a gender and stick to it.

"Fuck!" Dino announced when he finally came inside of her. She knew he was strapped with cash and didn't mind. Plus she was up three nuts to his one, so it was only right.

"Get up and get dressed!" He announced breathless.

"Excuse me?" Tonya reeled in disbelief. She just knew he wasn't about to chump her off like that.

"Go pack all your shit and come stay here with me!" He explained. That first piece of pussy was life changing.

Chapter Twenty-Eight

$\mathcal{A}$ camel is a strong muhfucka, but even it has its limits. So much so that when that limit is reached a mere straw can break its back. D-block was that camel and the gangs were the straws.

Trouble may have been free but the civilian population of D-block were anything but. With Lil-Zay at the wheel the Riders got on the fuck shit immediately. They were as soon just as bad as the Rollers and the whole prison was beginning to feel it. There were so many robberies the Riders and Rollers might fight each other for the right to rob someone.

The White boys had flourished under Rabbit but Rabbit was in a hole in the ground now. Ghost was muscle and muscle doesn't make good leadership. He didn't garner the same respect as Rabbit once did and the gang was falling apart. Losing the plug made them strictly consumers of their drug of choice. Without the income some turned to turning tricks to stay high. Some got a war daddy to support their habits, others banded with what was left of the Bandos.

The Bandos still maintained their solidarity but no one feared them once their one eyed monster had went home. Now they fell victim to both the Riders and the Rollers. They were robbed and beat up on a daily basis.

The Muslims kept to themselves under Shakur's leadership

but the gangs bullshit was causing chaos in the land. The prison was on and off lock-down every day from someone getting fucked up or stabbed up. Then came that final straw.

"Look, the world is ours! No one gave it to us, we took it! We Rollers, we takes what we want!" Rallo declared as his minions listened on in awe. His numbers grew with every arrival of new arrivals. "Now, Ion give a fuck what a muhfucka is, if he got something we want, we taking the shit!"

The pep talk on the yard was put in effect immediately. The Rollers spread out and began robbing anyone they came across. They obviously didn't see the Mexicans or the Muslims so they just robbed civilians. White, or black if they had it, the Rollers took it.

Lil-Zay wasn't a leader himself so he followed what he saw Rallo doing. He sent his Riders on a similar mission to take everything they could take.

"Hey shawty, run them headphones!" A Roller demanded and he and two others rolled up on and old man everyone called 'dad'. He had been riding longer than most people had been living but they didn't care.

"I need my headphones son," Dad pleaded. "I use them to listen to my gospel."

"Nigga!" One of the boys shouted and slapped the old man down. His headphones went one way while he went another. The crack of his hip seemed to press the pause button on the whole yard. Yup, that was that straw.

Each faction mumbled within itself, then with each other and a revolution was born.

～

"Look, tomorrow this shit is going to pop off. Just stay in the cell. Keep the door closed, and stay in!" Trouble warned as he came into the cell.

"The gangs planning some shit huh?" Darius guessed. An easy guess since they were always starting some shit.

"I just spoke to Rev. He got together with the Mexicans, Muslims, whites and anyone not affiliated. They're going to move on the Rollers tomorrow," he explained. "It's about to go down. People will die."

The Christians had more numbers than the rest of the faction put together. The former crack addict called Rev had the charisma to get them to finally stand up for themselves. Shakur accepted his proposal to rid the land of corruption. The Mexicans quickly signed on too since they too were being victimized.

The camel's back had officially broken. The battle lines had been drawn. A battle that supersedes race, religion and nation. In the end there are only two sides anyway. Good versus evil.

"You OK?" Trouble asked when he saw the troubled look on Darius's face. He knew the daily violence of the place unnerved him.

"Huh? Yeah!" He replied with an urgency Trouble couldn't register. "Can I make a call?"

"Ride out. I'm finna take a shower. Lord knows how long we gonna be on lock-down after this!" He replied. The riot of the ladies of D-block wasn't shit compared to the shit storm rolling their way. The death toll would be much higher.

Trouble knew he had to fight against the corruption he helped start. He had his knives brought to him and spent the night sharpening them to a razors edge. The put up man put them away for the night along with his phone.

∼

"CHOW CALL!" THE OFFICER ANNOUNCED BEFORE THE SUN GOT a chance to announce the day.

"Guess I'll go see what I can see," Trouble said so he could hear what there was to hear.

"Huh?" Darius asked down from the top bunk. Trouble could still hear the fear in his tone but had no idea it had kept him up all night.

"I said I'll bring you a biscuit," he said and headed out. Morning was always a good time to get things done in general. But especially plotting against the gangs since they stayed up all night and slept all morning. This is a good time to launch an individual attack but the coordinated effort worked better at yard call. The combined forces numbers would be far superior on the yard so they would wait.

Rev had his game face on as he led his brothers in prayer. Likewise, the Muslims were facing the east bowing and prostrating to the One who made the east, the west and every other thing known and unknown. The people of God turned to God for help with what was to come.

Trouble went around and quickly found that no one had punked out. It was going down at yard call. Plus the biscuits were pretty good so he grabbed some for himself and his bunk-mate. He would have to eat them all himself because when he returned to the cell it was empty.

"I ain't even mad at you bruh," Trouble remarked to his Darius's empty bunk. Quite a few people had sought protective custody as of late so he couldn't blame the man for wanting to stay safe. There's no shame in not being about that life. The harm comes when people pretend they are when they're not.

He pulled the jelly from his locker and smashed the biscuits, then went back to sleep. It was going to be a long day.

"DAMN!" THE OFFICER ANNOUNCED WHEN THE CALL FOR YARD call was answered by nearly everyone. He was used to seeing the usual suspects but today everyone came out. Even the blind man who had been robbed had a knife on him too. The Rollers robbed him too so he just asked to be pointed in their direction so he could stab someone.

Trouble had only one particular target in mind. He planned to pull the family card to get close to his cousin. Close enough to kill him. He could feel Rallo looking at him with that same smug smirk he wore since sowing the seeds of sedition that got him ousted from the gang. Not knowing he did him a huge favor.

The Riders and Rollers came out like always. They were high, hyped, animated and totally oblivious to the fact that some of them were dying today. All the other factions and groups were laser focused as they took their usual spots. The train came through at the same time every day. It blew its horn to announce its presence every day. This day it would announce a war. When it blew its horn today it would set off the battle for D-block.

"What the hell?" Warden Mays wondered when she looked down and saw over double the usual numbers on the yard. She was aleady stressing the loss in income from Rabbit, Dino and Trouble no longer at the helm of their respective gangs.

"Something ain't right!" Davis agreed and she was right. The words were barely out of her mouth before all hell broke loose. And the train hadn't even blown its horn yet.

"What the..." Someone said as they looked up and saw several helicopters from several directions nearing the prison. Everyone looking up diverted attention from the black vans barreling into the prison parking lot. Men dipped in all black everything, carrying black sub-machine guns piled out and surrounded the perimeter of the yard and aimed their weapons.

The helicopters got lower, dropping canisters of tear gas before landing. Men scrambled in the chaos but there was only one place to go. And only one alternative to going to that place.

"Everyone down! On your faces or you will be shot! Down! On your faces!" The men screamed and spread out. A few young ones needed help to the ground and got it. Some where tased, others shoved and a couple slammed on their faces.

"Did you call this?" Mays wondered to her security warden as they watched the scene unfold.

"Ion even know who they are!" She assured her. They both got the answers they sought when the office door was knocked off the hinges.

"Warden Mays you're under arrest! Deputy warden Davis,

you're under arrest!" The federal agents barked as they were put in cuffs.

Meanwhile the agents on the yard used zip ties to secure each man's feet and wrist. They were all rolled on the back to be identified. One agent did the identifying while others placed a different colored tag to designate affiliation.

"Roller. Roller. Rider," he was pointing out to the shock of those being pointed out. Darius and Trouble locked eyes before he said, "Civilian."

"I told y'all he was the police!" Bama cheered happily. He was delighted to be right since he remembered the face from the drug bust that got Trouble snitched on.

"Rider and Roller!" Darius announced over him and two tags were placed on him. Even though he was neither after being turned out by Dino.

"This nigga was a fed. The whole time. In my cell," Trouble sighed to himself and shook his head. Darius had witnessed him moving so much dope for the wardens and himself. His would be the strongest case of them all since he witnessed it first hand. Plus, he saw him rule the Riders up close and personal. Trouble was in big trouble.

The inmates sat out the yard for hours as they were sorted out by gang as well as charges. There were several other undercover agents in the prison and they were able to build strong cases. Rallo and the other gang bangers were in extra trouble with RICO charges as well as domestic terrorism for the gang ties.

They were read their rights on the new charges before being taking back inside for lock down. Usually the federal charges meant transfer to a federal facility but that wouldn't be necessary since the feds were taking over D-block. The various gangs were assigned to the same dorms and locked behind the door until they would see a judge. That would take a couple of years but didn't matter since they were faces decades for the charges.

Trouble was left out on the yard with the other civilians well after nightfall while the entire prison was rearranged to meet the new standard. He and Darius locked eyes a few times but didn't get to speak. It was only once the yard cleared that they had the chance to trade quick one liners in passing.

"Told you I owed you one," Darius said from the corner of his mouth like a ventriloquist. Fed or not, he liked the young man. Plus Trouble saved his life. This was his chance to return the favor.

"Thank you," Trouble announced. Darius may have been undercover but the conversations were real. They really got to know each other and formed a bond. A bond that saved him at least another decade behind these walls.

Chapter Twenty-Nine

"*I* wish I ain't even have this damn baby!" Malaysia groaned to the absolute shock to the doctor and nurses around the room to deliver the baby.

"Hush chile don't say that!" Granny fussed at her. Not that she disagreed since the girl certainly didn't need another child. Especially since the first child was still at her house.

"It's true! The daddy dead, I'm all alone. Fuck I need with another damn baby!" She snarled.

"You know what..." One of the nurses announced and began to remove her gear on the way out of the room. "I can't..."

"I'm gonna need to clear the room so we can perform a c-section," the doctor announced and cleared the room. Granny shook her head the whole way out. She already knew she would end up raising that child just like she raised the mother and the mother before.

The procedure was successful and produced a healthy baby boy. He was named after the father he would never know. Malaysia was stitched up and sent home to mope with the new baby. Granny sent the younger girls to 'spina night so she wouldn't be alone. Postpartum depression is a beast but Malaysia made it worse by self medicating.

"About dang time!" She sang fondly as she lit a blunt for the first time in months. She wasn't the best mother but not the worst either and hung up the smoking and drinking until she delivered. Right until she delivered because she had a one day old in the living room with her little cousins while she was in the bedroom blazing.

Malaysia decided to post some pics of her and Pablo's baby on her social media but got sidetracked. Seeing her friends living their best lives while she had been couped up depressed her even further. Tootie now had over two million followers just from being Doobie Daddies girlfriend. A picture of her ultrasound had hundreds of thousands of 'likes' in minutes and she knew she was fucking with that.

Day by day she slipped further into depression and despair. The drugs and alcohol only made matters worse but the worst was yet to come. It rang the doorbell when it did come.

"Lay-lay! The 'do!" The girls yelled as the door bells chime.

"That's Jaquita! Let her in!" She called back from the steamy bathroom.

"Heeeeey!" Jaquita sang and twerked as she entered the apartment. The poor little girls were so used to piss poor role models they began to twerk along with her. And they didn't even have nothing to twerk yet.

"Go to my room!" Malaysia called from the bedroom. She had to rushed to wrap it up since Jaquita will steal something.

"Hey girl!" Jaquita greeted when she rushed into the room.

"Hey girl. I'm ready to get fucked up and get my groove on!" She swore. She already smoked a blunt and drank a few beers but Jaquita was ready to up the ante.

"Dis what you need!" She said and produced a package of white powder. The girl was a dope boy's girl her whole life and knew exactly what it was. Malaysia watched her dump some on the dresser and form several lines. She snorted two of them and backed away.

There really should have been some thought given to such

a important decision but there wasn't. Malaysia leaned in and inhaled the others right away. As if this were the moment she had been waiting for.

Rick James once said 'cocaine is a helluva drug. He was right too because tonight was the first night of what would be every night for a long time to come. Jaquita knew her friend was sitting on swole so getting her on the powder was investment in the future of her getting high.

The investment really paid off when Malaysia eventually dropped the new baby off to her granny so she could get her party on properly. They would go on to hit every club in Atlanta, every night of the week.

～

"Clayton, Trevor. Visitation," a federal officer announced from the booth. They had completely taken over and replaced the state officers. Some had been reassigned while others had been arrested.

"Your grandmother?" Trouble's new bunk-mate, Steven asked when Trouble's name was called.

"Yup!" He happily announced. With the feds running the joint he didn't have the luxury of talking to her the whole way down but since she was the only one who came to visit it was an easy guess.

The phones had actually survived the massive shake down that came with the takeover but the prison was still on lock down months later so there was no way to get to them. Whenever they came off lock-down the newly installed cameras would prevent them from being retrieved anyway.

The gentlemen of D-block were doing hard time behind the door. Even the GED class work was delivered to the dorm and slid under the door. Trouble actually thrived in the new environment since he could focus.

It took months after the seize before limited visits were allowed. They were only for the civilians not awaiting trials on everything ranging from conspiracy to murder and everything in between. The wardens as well as the the female officers indicted in the various crimes were taken to a female facility. Including pussy by the pound, except for Jessie who got out before shit hit the fan.

"This the part I hate," Trouble groaned when he was pulled aside to be stripped before his visit.

It's unknown if anyone has ever sent contraband out of a prison through visitation but the degradation was worth hearing little Trevor say 'daddy'. He would be stripped again on his way back inside but his days of being a dope boy were over. His new bunk-mate Steven built websites until a bad decision landed him in jail for a spell. It was just another source for Trouble to learn from and he soaked up all he could from the man. It was an even swap since Trouble taught him some swag to help him with the ladies.

"You can get dressed again," the federal officer said professionally after looking up his ass. The professionalism was a big switch from the state officers. Several inmates caught more charges trying to bribe them to bring in contraband. It took months before the prison population got the picture. Those days were over. Prison was no longer fun. Being associated with the gangs was no longer fun once the gang charges were added in. They called for sentence enhancements that added ten years to run with whatever they got. Not to mention that time would be served in high max.

"Hey there lady!" Trouble greeted when he spotted his beloved in the half filled waiting list. His son stood on his own, holding his hands to be picked up.

"Hey there baby!" She cooed with the new baby boy in her arms. Trouble kissed her fluffy cheek as he scooped his son up. He raspberried his cheek and made him crack up.

"That's ole girl baby?" He asked even though he knew the answer. Granny just shook her head in fear of what would come out if she opened it. She hadn't seen Malaysia since she dropped the new baby off. "Heard from cuz?"

"Chile..." She said and shook her head. She hadn't heard correctly from Rallo but did recently speak with his lawyer.

"How much time they talking?" He asked and shook her head some more.

"The rest of it! They done charged him with drugs, murder, assault, err thing!" She said without a trace of sorrow. People aren't usually sad when people get what they deserve. The hit he sent Fuck-shit on came back to haunt him when he agreed to testify. Rallo had already been under investigation so they spared the kid to testify against him. Over a hundred members of his gang had turned state against him.

Most of the Riders tried to snitch on Trouble but Darius insisted he wasn't an official member of the gang. Just loosely associated from growing up with them but not an actual member. Lil-Zay was the next best thing so they all told on him. Trouble should have warned him of the weight of that crown but he wanted it so bad.

Ghost dumb ass got himself murder charges for bragging about having Rabbit wacked. Most of the White boys agreed to testify against him but he was the best witness against himself for sharing that picture. Fitz made sure to have some money put on his books for diverting any blame away from him.

"Well," Trouble shrugged at the news. It was nothing compared to the news she would have gotten if the riot had popped off since he planned to kill Rallo. "They got some jalapeño burgers in there?"

"Yeah, hole him," she said and passed the baby off before he could object.

"Baby," little Trevor smiled as his daddy held Malaysia and Pablo's love child. It was actually therapeutic and helped him mentally move on. He didn't even return him when granny returned with his food and drink.

"I just hope she still got my bread," Trouble said wistfully, like he didn't believe it himself.

"Hmp!" She huffed since she knew first hand how hard Malaysia was balling. She was on her third car in four months since she didn't appreciate shit enough to take care of shit. The Telsa had been wrecked and she didn't have insurance.

That lead to her using Trouble's Caddy until it was stolen. A police report could have gotten it back but she never filed one. Just bought the Lexus she was pushing now. Plus, cocaine is a helleva drug.

"Well, I got a letter from the parole board. A federal agent wrote a letter on my behalf. They took a year off my parole date," he sighed. It wasn't as good as immediate release but it was better than nothing.

"That's wonderful baby!" She purred even though it was still a couple years away. It was just long enough to turn the boy into a man.

ASSOCIATES DEGREE IN BUSINESS. THE BUILDING BLOCK EVERY entrepreneur can benefit from.

"OK now look. When you start feeling all tingly in your legs, that's when you pull that thang out! Just snatch it out!" Another officer laughed as he led Trouble to the last door between him and his freedom.

"Believe it or not, that's not that high on my list," Trouble sighed. He was a male and males love pussy, but he was also a man and men keep things in their proper perspective. The officer nodded in admiration of the man and watched him walk to his family.

"Daddy!" Little Trevor shouted and took off running. His brother Pablo said the same and did the same since Trouble was the only father he had known up until then. They had bonded during the weekly visits just like he was his own.

"Hey y'all!" Trouble smiled back and bent low to scoop them up. He did and squealed just as loudly as them when he twirled them around. He could see the wide smile on his grandmother's face as he did. Hers wasn't the only familiar face he had seen. He sat the boys down and told them, "Go to Granny. I'll be right there."

"No," both boys refused, shaking their little heads. No way were they letting daddy get away again.

"Alright. Come on," he laughed and took them with him.

Part of him wanted to ignore her but another part needed an explanation. There was a lot less of the person, but the face remained the same.

"Here," Jessie began and handed him a thick manila envelope. He could smell the brand new hundreds without even opening it. "It's all there. Fifty two thousand dollars."

"OK, thanks," he said through the lump in his throat. He had given up all hopes of seeing a penny of the money he made in prison. His ear was no longer to the streets after the feds took over but he didn't have any delusions of Malaysia doing right. Jessie turned back to her fancy truck to leave but Trouble had a question. "What happened?"

"You did," she said as her lip began to quiver. She quickly caught herself and explained. "You talked so crazy to me that last time, I felt like dirt. But, you was right! I am better than that! I on know how I got sucked into that life but you insulted me enough to change for the better."

"I was drunk tho," he offered in excuse for his bad behavior.

"Drunk tongue speak a sober mind!" She reminded. "It was true tho. I was going out bad. But I took my lil money and opened a daycare. Then a restaurant. Lost weight, got God."

"Well, I'm glad things worked out for the better," he said sincerely. They shared a smile and turned to head back to their lives.

Trouble was holding each son by the hand as he walked over to his grandmother. Everyone was all smiles until two men stepped from a waiting car. Neither wore a smile but they both wore the trademark Fedora of Atlanta homicide detectives.

"Trevor Clayton?" One asked even though they all knew.

"Yeah. Go to Granny. Take this," he said to them and his sons.

"Come on boys! Yo daddy finna ride with his friends! He right behind us!" She demanded to kill their protest. The detectives had enough heart to let them pull off before putting Trouble in cuffs.

"Sorry lil bruh, we gotta take you in on a murder charge," the other detective said as he helped him into the backseat. He was doing his job but even he didn't like how that just went down.

Trouble just shrugged and exercised his right to remain silent. One of the lessons he learned in prison was that it is what it is. Whatever it is. There wasn't a bitch ass thing he could say at the moment to make anything any different so he enjoyed the scenery as it whipped by the window.

"HE SAY ANYTHING?" THE LEAD DETECTIVE ASKED ONCE THEY arrived at the station. Trouble had been tucked into an interview room waiting to be interviewed.

"Not a word? Never even asked what this was about?" One of the detectives squinted.

"Because he already knows!" The boss barked.

"Yeah but unless he admits it we ain't got shit on him. Certainly can't put a drugged out stripper on the stand," the other added.

"Well, get in there and get him to admit it!" Their boss demanded. Both sighed and turned to interrogate the suspect in the years old homicide.

"Sorry about the wait!" One said as the other asked, "Thirsty?"

"No problem," Trouble replied for them to share.

"Look, we're just trying to figure out what happened with you and Nut?" One asked.

"Err body say y'all was cool?" The other added.

Trouble remained cool as the proverbial cucumber on the outside but his heart stopped when he heard the name of the only thing he hadn't answered for yet. That same heart threatened to break when he realized the only person who could have told on him. Malaysia made sure no one else did by killing Ridell. Now it was she linking him to the case. The three detectives watched hopefully as the wheels turned in Trouble's head.

"Come on mother fucker! Come clean you son of a bitch!" The supervisor cheered as he watched in the monitor from the next room. So many times they brought in a suspect they had nothing on in hopes he would give them something. It was amazing how many ran their mouths and talked themselves into a murder charge. They almost lost hope in Trouble doing the same until his mouth began to slowly open.

"You want to hear about a murder? OK, I'll tell you about a murder..." Trouble began.

∾

"DADDY!" THE BOYS CHEERED ONCE AGAIN WHEN THEIR father walked into the house. They rushed for a hug but Granny shoved them aside and got to him first.

"Oh my god! Are you OK boy!" She shrieked and engulfed him into a grandmother hug.

"I, c,c,cain't, breathe," he gasped and she let him out the deadly hold.

"What them folks wanted?" She demanded as she inspected him for damages.

"Misunderstanding. Err thing good," he assured her and hugged the boys. "Did you cook?"

"You know I did!" She proudly proclaimed since she didn't just cook. She showed the fuck out.

Trouble followed her into the kitchen and sat down. Granny piled his plate high with her famous macaroni and cheese, fried chicken, collards greens....

Several hours had passed before Trouble awoke from the food induced coma. Ironically it was in the same bed this story began. Except this time it was one of his own sons who peed on him. Being back home wasn't a disappointment since he at least had a place to start from.

Trouble had earned hundreds of thousands of dollars in the streets and chain gang but it was almost all gone now. He did have plenty of good ideas and a few legit contacts from his time in prison. Even Darius told him to call when he got home. The future was brighter than it had ever been but there was still one more door from his past that needed to be closed. He got up to go close it.

"Can I use your car Granny?" He asked from her doorway.

"Sure you can baby," she readily agreed since she knew he needed to handle his business. "When you start to feel tingly, snatch that thang out!"

Trouble just shook his head and laughed as he headed out. Nothing much had changed in the hood. Not even the faces really since sons took their daddy's spot on these same corners. A slight snarl lifted the corner of his lip at the thought of little Trevor following in his footsteps. He planned to get him and little Pablo out first chance he got. The fifty grand he had was a good start.

"Hmp," Trouble huffed as he pulled into the parking lot of the Chili Pepper. He knew exactly what was inside and that's why he stayed outside. The side door of the club opened and he saw who he came to see. Malaysia looked a lot older than the years that had passed as she came out. Some of that was because of the fast life she had been living. Some was due to a homicide detective on each arm.

"Ion know what the fuck y'all 'talmbout! I ain't kilt no damn Ridell!" She fussed and kicked as she was taken out in cuffs.

"We got a witness say otherwise!" One said. Trouble never admitted to Nut's murder but didn't mind giving Malaysia up for killing Ridell. He was in police custody when it went down so it could never be put back on him.

Malaysia ran her mouth the whole way to the station and again once she got inside. She told on a bunch of hood shit she heard of by the hood niggas she dealt with. She eventually told on herself and was booked on the murder charge. And that's how the story ends....

The End

The aftermath

THE FALLOUT FROM THE FUCKERY AT D-BLOCK WASN'T SWIFT but it was brutal. First there was Rallo who finally got what he deserved. Two separate death sentences for two different murders. He didn't kill anyone with his own hands but his Rollers snitched on him for the ones he ordered along with a few he hadn't. Even the three of the shooters who shot Pablo snitched on him to reduce their own time. Not to mention several life sentences for being the leader of the gang.

GHOST GOT A DEATH SENTENCE HIMSELF BUT ARGUED HE should get a deal too since it was his own bragging that convicted him. He had sent the text and picture to so many people it was like him testifying against himself. The judge don't agree and sentenced his dumb ass to death.

LIL-ZAY WANTED TO BE THE BIG MAN AND GOT TREATED AS such. One of those 'be careful what you wish for' moments. As the leader of the Riders he was charged with each crime each Rider was charged with. Including some that happened on the streets since he was the king. The gang enhancements with each charge cost him more time than he had coming to him in . The several life sentences and hundreds of years meant he would die in prison. Then, he would still be on parole in his grave. If it seems like everyone snitched on everyone else it's only because they did. That's the reality of the streets that they don't rap about.

BOTH WARDENS WERE CONVICTED OF RUNNING A CONTINUING criminal enterprise and given lengthy prison sentences. They made more money than they knew how to hide and the government swooped in and took every cent. The only thing worst than being in prison is being broke in prison.

MALAYSIA TALKED HERSELF INTO A MURDER CHARGE BUT WAS able to bargain herself ten years for manslaughter since she told on several crimes she heard through pillow talk. It turned out to be a blessing since the sobriety allowed her to see things clearer. She enrolled in GED as well as bible study and was one her way to turning her life around.

DINO AND TONYA MARRIED SHORTLY AFTER MOVING IN together. They eventually needed a bigger house once they began to have a baby a year for the next five years. His good looks got him good money as a male model. After that first shot of girl pussy he never went back to boy pussy.

TROUBLE ABANDONED HIS NICKNAME AND STAYED OUT OF trouble. Darius kept his word and they went into business together flipping houses. He took to legit business just as well as he did the street life. The single women loved the single dad but he took his time looking for his soul mate. Pablo's mom came and claimed her grandson once the DNA proved his lineage. Trouble still picked him up on weekends so the brothers could grow up together.

STACK HAD STACKED ENOUGH MONEY IN HIS THIRTY YEARS behind the wall to retire once he got home. He could be found whipping along on his motorcycle up and down Cascade or bouncing a grand baby on his knee.

SA'ID SALAAM HAD HIS CASE OVERTURNED AND FELL OFF THE face of the earth. Rumor has it he's living in a hut in Africa with a monkey and a parrot. He was never heard from again but does still drop a book from time to time. So the end was really just the beginning.

CHECK OUT SOME HEAT FROM MY PARTNERS DESHION (STACK Cascade) Hightower and The Executive Homeboy...

Shit Just Got Real

**An excerpt from
the
Executive Homeboy**

Prologue

ace to face with Houston's Saturday night skies, Triple J, sat relaxing outdoors in a soft cushioned rose red patio chair. The weather was even tempered, perfect for relaxing outside on a Saturday night. He and his wife, Mrs. Jessica Reeves-Johnson, were supposed to be traveling under the radar, but she picked the number one hotel in the city of Houston to spend the night.

Spoiled to her core, Jessica refused to sleep in anything less than the five-star rating hotel. So tonight, they're spending it at the hotel Grandaca Houston. Usually when they traveled, Triple J made sure they were protected by at least thirty members of his Ape's and Wolves crew. Mainly members from the hunters, his cleanup crew, but tonight, it's just the two of them.

Triple J knew he wasn't supposed to move in such manner, because it put them both in a physical danger. The streets don't have a heart and big fish like Triple J had enemies they didn't even know existed.

The trip to Texas was scheduled as a day trip—fly in, check on her grandfather, and fly right back to Atlanta, but in the midst of their visit, Bianca, Jessica's favorite cousin, showed up out of the blue. What a coincidence it was Bianca was also there to surprise Grandpa at the same time that they did.

"Growing up, Jessica and Bianca were inseparable," their grandfather told Triple J. "And even though they're cousins, you would think they were twins. Can you believe this one year, they both sent me the same shirt for Christmas and the only difference in the whole gift was the name on the top of the box? They think just alike," Grandpa chuckled.

Now for the first time in five years, they're seeing of each other Triple J learned and the surprise visit had them super excited. Jessica had been super busy with Triple J and the day-to-day operations in their real estate group, while Bianca had been engulfed in her work at a high-paying government job she had out in Cali.

Jessica never told Triple J what exactly Bianca did because she knew how he felt about Feds. All he knew was she traveled a lot. For Jessica, the trip to see grandpa was a bit of bitter-sweet. She loved them both and wished for them all to hang out, but Triple J couldn't. What most people didn't know was for a major player in the streets like he was, shit got real. Crossing over state lines into other territories for business or vacation, meant he must check in. The rule said that if one was traveling outside of his approved travel space, he must notify the family's Chief of Security of the departure, who covered the territory in which he visited. Once he did so, the family's Chief of Security could grant permission or rejection before he arrived. Triple J had done neither and Jessica acted as if she didn't understand why he said they had to remain low-key before they'd left Atlanta.

"When we travel outside of the United States, the government requires us to have visas. The streets are the same way," he told her.

Just to make this trip, had already cost him 170k in flight expenses. To keep it off all stations, he had to make a couple of mint rich calls and settled on a business deal he had no plans of settling for another month. The Learjet was loaned out by one of his personal business associates so they could bypass airport TSA and arrive there under false names.

Pouting because she couldn't spend the night out with her favorite two, Jessica sped around their hotel suite with her lips poking out, slinging her backside in every direction from underneath her turquoise lace boy shorts. From his view, Triple J thought, *She looks like one of those big stank booty strippers at a hole in the wall strip club that ain't made no money all night.*

Can you say attitude!

Never did he enjoy seeing her upset, but he did think the walk was kind of cute as she stumped her way into the bathroom.

While Jessica was getting dolled up, Triple J enjoyed the stress-free moment before she'd interrupted him.

"Daddy!" she called out, walking from their apartment sized bathroom. "Does this dress look slutty?" she asked.

Triple J turned towards her and walked through the glass slide door. Standing in front of him, he stared in amazement.

Oh my God. She looks like a beauty queen, he thought.

Jessica only wore the best and if she were into pageants, she could have easily won Miss America. Modeling for him, she wore a purple custom-made Michael Kors, gold studded uneven hem dress that cut knee level. She stood offset with her right leg slightly advanced, showing off the contour of her body.

Dressed elegantly with all of the matching Michael Kors gold accessories, necklace, bracelet, and time watch, she gave him a cold shiver that raced across every vertebrate of his spine. Styled by H0n3y @HoneyLegacy in Atlanta, Jessica stayed dressed in only the best of attire each time she stepped out, putting on for her city.

As Triple J continued to stare her down, wild thoughts ran through his mind.

It's like God created her for himself, he thought.

Hands down, Mrs. Jessica Reeves-Johnson was made for a king and just by the luck of the draw, he got her. Running his eyes across her body, Triple J wondered why she asked if her dress looked slutty. Honey's Nation seamstress hemmed it perfectly, hugging her curves like a mother with her child for the first time.

Triple J saw nothing wrong, but if the U.S. Department of Transportation inspectors saw her, they would. An emergency order would be sent to the State Governor, forcing them to put up warning signs around Jess because the curves ahead were sharp.

"You look beautiful baby," he said. "Why would you even ask me do you look slutty?," Triple J asked as he walked up to her licking his lips. Jessica giggled as Triple J reached out grabbing her right hand.

"No, I"m serious, daddy. Does it look slutty?" she asked him for a second time.

Head held high, she stared at a 45-degree angle, showing off her beautiful jawline as she waited for him to respond. Rocking from side to side, she mimicked a runway model that would pause at the edge of the stage.

"You're beautiful and it's beautiful," he said with amazement in his eyes. "It fits you love. I can see Mrs. Michelle Obama wanting to wear this dress after seeing you in it."

"Really? You think the First Lady would wanna wear a dress like me?"

"Without a shadow of doubt! She won't look as good as you do, but absolutely." he said, lifting her hand above her head before spinning her slowly like a ballerina.

Jessica blushed as she turned, harder than he'd ever seen her blush. Much harder than she did when they had first met.

She broke away from his grip and lifted both hands up, grabbing around his neck. Rising on the tip of her toes, she lifted up to his lips and kissed him with her luscious lips. Twirling in circles, she caught his between her teeth, biting down slightly before she released his as she pulled away. Licking up his face as she pulled way, she left a wet spot on the tip of his nose.

"Daddy, I love you so much," she said. "You've always made me feel special. Even on a night like tonight."

"I know you want me to come, but really I can't," he said to her.

Jessica interlocked fingers with him and they both stared silently deep into each other's eyes. Her big and beautiful brown eyes gave a glow so beautiful, that Triple J lit up each time he stared into them.

Holding hands, they both recognized that their love for one another was way deeper than any of them can understand. Their connection reached deep, way into the crevices of the soul.

Jessica's phone rang, interrupting their romantic moment and they both knew who the call came from.

"Hey, B," Jessica said as she answered the phone. "Okay, I'm on the way down now sis," she continued after a slight pause.

Grabbing the extra magazine to his pistol from between the sofa's cushion, Triple J quickly slid it in his back pocket as she slid on her heels. "Will you ride down the elevator with me?" she asked after checking her makeup one last time.

"Yeah, baby. You don't think I was gonna let you ride down by yourself, did you?"

"I don't know. You know you have them street rules you have to follow. Rule number three says you can't walk your wife downstairs or open the car door," she said sarcastically.

"Watch out," Triple J said, brushing her sarcasm off.

Stepping out of the room, they held hands to the elevator. Triple J stepped in behind his wife and placed his back against the wall. Jessica backed against him, pressing her butt on his lap as they rode down to the lobby.

As the doors opened, Jess gave him three pecks on the lips.

"I love you, daddy," she said before stepping off.

Triple J stayed on the elevator but watched as she walked away.

Her walk away was breath taking switched up and down every time she stepped. Jessica knew he was watching because as the elevator doors beeped before closing, she twirled around, flung her hair, then smiled as she continued to march away.

My bitch bad, Triple J thought, as he rode the elevator up alone.

Bored out of this world, Triple J dozed off after flipping through channels when he got back in the room. The suite's door opened, and he quickly grabbed his custom Glock 23 compact .40 cal, aiming its barrel towards the hotel suite's door as it opened.

"Baby, it's me," Jessica said, announcing herself as she walked in.

Triple J lowered his gun and checked his wristwatch for the time, because the night still felt young. Next he grabbed his cell phone off the nightstand, checking it for any missed calls because he knew usually, Jessica would have called or texted, letting him know that she was on her way back, but tonight she didn't.

"Damn, it's just 10:35," he said to himself, but loud enough so she could hear him. It was a sure thing that if they were home, she would have hung out at least until 2:30 or 3:00 AM.

Something's not right, Triple J thought to himself.

"What's up, pretty lady?" he asked as he walked up to Jessica stepping out of her shoes," Did you enjoy yourself," he asked.

Jess didn't respond but let out a sigh like she was upset.

"What time do the clubs close out here?" he asked her, looking at his watch again.

"We didn't go to a club. They were all overcrowded, so we just hit up a restaurant, talked and sipped wine," she said with a slight slur in her speech.

"What's wrong, Jessie? Were y'all not having a good time?"

"You don't miss me?" she asked quickly with a hint of anger in her voice.

"Of course, I miss you! I'm just trying to figure out what's got my smile upset."

"Daddy! We did have a good time. Maybe I came back early because I had to tee-tee," Jessica said with a smirk on her face.

With only one heel off, Jessica stood with her legs crossed like a little kid rocking back and forth doing the pee-pee dance.

"You hell," Triple J replied, laughing at her drunkard

behavior. "Go pee and don't get none my floor," he continued, laughing at her move quickly for the bathroom.

Bouncing up and down as she walked in one heel, he stopped her in her tracks outside the bathroom door.

"Baby, let me help you take off your heel," he said, bending down reaching for her foot, being the gentleman that he was.

Deep down though she knew he really loved her and ensuring her safety was his job. No real man would watch his wife continue down the path of disaster and possibly twist her ankle. Triple J returned to the bed and laid back. All night long, he'd been chilling, and his phone hadn't rung one time, surprisingly, until she got back. The incoming call came from the encrypted telephone app he had for close relatives during emergencies only. So immediately his antennas raised.

"Papa, what's up?" he answered the call quickly, coming from the old man, Pastor James Johnson, Senior.

"Where you at, son?" he asked in a very serious tone.

"Texas with Jess. What's going on?"

"Stay put. Atlanta homicide detectives just came by looking for you."

"Was it just the detectives or the whole team?" Triple J asked.

"Errbody," his father said sadden, "They came deep."

Lost for words Triple J remained silent. His whole world had been shaken up and that's when he knew then, Shit Just Got Real.

Love Always

_____

An excerpt from
Deshion Hightower

Chapter Thirty

"*B*aboy, take this ten and go get a loaf of bread. Don't forget to get you something sweet, his grandmother told him with a warm smile.

Like always, he automatically knew when grandma gave him money to go to the store, the change would be him. She didn't have to tell him to keep the change but she did anyway. He would stop by the arcade game room to play some games and look at the girls though.

Baboy went to the store he'd been going in since he was a git. He was 13 years old and was big for his age. He stood 5'9 and wore 171 pounds. He couldn't wait to get out of middle school and start high school. He wasn't interested in middle school anymore, he wanted to see what the big girls were about in high school.

When he pulled the ten dollar bill out someone behind him snatched the money. His mouth fell open in shock. *God, I hope this is one of my friends playing,* he thought to himself. The owner of the store Mr. Jessie ran from behind the counter, opened the door and began to scream very loud.

"Jerry, bring this kid back his money now!" Old man Jessie knew baboy when he was an arm baby. He also knew his entire family. Baboy was a good kid to him. Baboy got caught stealing a buggy full of meat from Kroger and another time the word was he had stolen a few cars. It didn't matter because there wasn't any truth to it nor proof. He was an only child to his mom. Mr. Jessie taught him how to cut meat in his store.

Jerry stood there with his big arms folded staring at Baboy. He was a football player in high school standing 6'5 245 pounds. Baboy didn't know whether to run or shit on himself. He stopped ten feet away from Jerry. He was scared to look away or down. He thought of what his dad and grandfather always told him. Always look a man in his eyes. His mind told him to run but his heart said Rayshawn don't be no coward. You ain't no hoe so take this ass whooping or give it.

He thought, *pick up something and beat this bitch, if not he gonna kill me.* "Hey man, let me get my grandma money man," he asked in a soft tone of voice.

"Nigga, fuck you and yo granny," said Jerry looking at Baboy.

Baboy's blood was boiling. He quickly scanned the rocky parking lot with his thirsty mad eyes. He was done talking about it, right then and there. *Fuck my grandma,* he thought to himself. "Ok." He couldn't go home without his grandmother's bread.

Jerry looked in his eyes. "C'mon ya lil punk ass nigga."

Damn, he thought to himself. *This fool gone kill me over ten lil dollars.* What would God do? he thought. He could hear his grandma crying over his casket, 'ten dollars not worth your life baby.' He peeped his surroundings, it was bricks and broken bottles laid out all around the small rocky parking lot.

He reached down and picked up a small beer bottle and swang it as hard as he could to hit Jerry in the face. It only made the big man mad. He shook it off and ran at Baboy. He picked up another bottle running from the big monster looking guy. He leaned into Jerry and hit him hard. Blood started gushing from Jerry but he kept coming towards him as he was bleeding bad. Baboy picked up a red brick and swung it hard as he could and hit him in the middle of the face. Jerry fell face first on the concrete. When he fell, Baboy went to stomp his head and kicked him in the belly. Jerry rolled over so

Bboy wouldn't kick him in his face so he kicked him dead in the ass.

"Fuck you pussy nigga! Never disrespect my grandma or me sucka," he said as he stuck his hand in Jerry's jean pocket and came out with two hundred plus his grandma's ten. He stuck it in his pocket and went back to the store.

Old Man JB owned the club across the street from Mr. Jessie's store and watched the kid stand his ground with Jerry. Not to mention,the kid defeated the coward bully. He saw Jerry take lots of people money because of his size. That's how he took care of his habits. JB instantly took a liking to Baboy. He had a smirk on his face from what he just witnessed. JB cleaned his windows and watched Baboy go back in the store.

Mr. Jessie gave Baboy the brown paper bag with the bread in it. "Listen son, you could have gotten hurt. Now get whatever you need and run along. I gotta call the police cause he don't look like he's getting up by himself. They will ask me who did it, but I gotcha back on that part son. Go home and stay outta trouble."

"Yes sir Mr. Jessie," he said as he handed Mr. Jessie the ten.

"No son, keep it and run along now. And son, go the back way home.'

"Yes sir," he said. He jumped on his bike taking the quickest way home up Cascade through the back pathway on Olympian and his monster bike in his mom's basement.

He sat at the dinner table with his grandfather James. He had just got off work from driving 18 wheelers. It was the same job he had for thirty-four years.

"Hey my boy," said his granddaddy, pulling his ear like he always did.

His grandfather was his best friend. He learned all his work trades from his grandfather. How to work on motors, do anything on cars, build just about anything you could name.He could also pour concrete and he knew how to weld. Baboy had lots of skills already at almost fourteen years of age. He learned it all from his father and grandfather.

Baboy was very nervous about what happened two hours ago. All kinds of crazy thoughts ran through his young mind. What if Jerry died? Then he'd be back in juvenile or in prison like his Uncle Stack. *Mom gone be mad at me. She just told me yesterday if I don't do the right thing and stay in school she will put me out. Dang,* he thought. *Where I'ma go because it's about to go down.*

Grandma brought out two plates of hot food and that took his mind off of all the bad things that was running his young mind crazy. His Grandma could throw down in the kitchen. She made fried chicken, collard greens, mac and cheese, candied yams, and that good ole pan cornbread in the burned pan on the stove. The food was smoking hot.

While biting into his juicy chicken he thought of his father. His dad loved to come over his grandparents house to eat. Baboy had never got the chance to meet his dad's parents. His dad passed away a year ago from a heart attack. He missed his dad. They were very close. His father had learned a lot of his skills from Mr. James, Baboy's grandfather. He was a jack of all trades and Baboy was all eyes and ears learning also. His father Harold had passed very young at 37 years old. He worked and was a real hustler to the end. He kept two jobs at all times. He sold moonshine and shot dice all over Georgia. Baboy remembered the times his dad would take him to dice games with him all over Atlanta, Griffin, Milledgeville, Macon, and Rome. He would ride with his dad to sell shine.

Baboy would fall asleep and when he woke up his shoes would be filled with hundreds. Those were the good times he had with his father. He had all the expensive clothes and shoes, watches, anything that he wanted. Since his dad had passed things changed. One night while he was asleep he heard some loud bumping and a sound like someone was crying. He got out of bed, walked down thehall and peeped in his dad's room. His pop's was standing on the floor fucking Pam like a dog. He turned to walk away but Pops caught him. He smiled at him and waved at him and told him to come on. Baboy ran and jumped in the bed scared as hell. His dad came and got him.

"Rashawn, come on, I want you to know what it's like to

went out or whatever they did together. He missed his dad. That was his true hero just like his grandfather. He never wanted for anything when his dad was alive. He had all the latest games, phones, whatever he wanted.

His mom worked at a hotel making ten dollars an hour. They were always behind on bills and the struggle was real now. He wanted to find a way to help his mom so bad. He ate all his meals over his grandparents house, right across the street from his mom's house.

He was full as a tick ready to shower and lay down so he hugged his grandma and grandpa and went across the street to his mom's house. He unlocked the door with his key and looked around the old empty crib. They had an outdated old colored TV, a wooden two seater sofa, and a wooden chair. He sat on the long sofa that was at least thirty years old. When he flopped down dust came up. He almost choked.

"Dang," he said.His day was a long one so he laid back and closed his eyes.

He thought he was dreaming when he heard his mother's voice.

"Baboy," she said.

"Hey mama," he said as he opened his eyes and got up and hugged her. She was smiling like she always was. Happy to see her only son.

He went to his room and laid across his old small bunk bed. He was looking at his walls with all the Run DMC posters, old pictures of him and his cousins and other family. The phone began to ring, the only phone they had was in the kitchen hanging over the stove. He had an iPhone that he had stolen out of a car though. The phone rang again.

"I got it mom," he said but when he made it to the kitchen his mom was already talking to someone. He heard his name something about a fight and he already knew what it was. "That damn Jerry," he said in a low voice.

"Rashawn!" his mom called at the top of her voice. When she called his real name it was trouble.

"Yes ma'am."

"Don't be Jeffing now."

"Mama I always say yes ma'am to you. Why would you say I'm tap dancing and Jeffing now?" He could tell she was upset because her teeth were close together very tight when she was talking looking mean and funny.

"What was you doing fighting a twenty-four year old man three times bigger than you for today?"

"Mom, I went to Mr. Jessie for grandma and that fool tried to take my money from me so I bust his ass."

"Ok, you bust his ass alright. He's in a coma and his brother and cousins are looking for you to hurt you as we speak. I'm calling you a cab and sending you to your Aunt Mary's house."

"Oh no mom, no disrespect but I'm not running from them or nobody else. I was in the right so whatever they got in mind for me I got something for them. Your son is not a coward and I'm not running Mama."

"Rashawn they bury the dead not the scared."

"Mama, I refuse to run. I was in the right so I'm standing on that. No, if you don't want me here I will go stay with Grandpa and grandma."

"Rashan, I just don't want to lose my only child."

"Mom,I'ma be ok. Please let me stay right here in Cascade," he said to his mom looking like his dad with a baby face.

"Okay son, I'm going to pray for us."

"Thanks mom, I love you." He hugged his mother and went into his room and started playing on his iPhone til his mom fell asleep. He creeped out the front door, locked it and went into his granddad's storage house. He had the keys to everything his granddad owned. He reached into a blue toolbox and pulled a black .38 snubnose out. Locked the storage house, went back into the house with six rounds in the loaded gun. He would explain if his granddad asked for it.

www.ingramcontent.com/pod-product-compliance
Lightning Source LLC
Chambersburg PA
CBHW060432180626
46817CB00007B/2777